The Name on the Wall

ALSO BY HERVÉ LE TELLIER

The Anomaly

All Happy Families

Atlas Inutilis

Eléctrico W

Enough About Love

The Intervention of a Good Man

The Sextine Chapel

A Thousand Pearls (for a Thousand Pennies)

The Name on the Wall

HERVÉ LE TELLIER

Translated from the French by
ADRIANA HUNTER

Other Press
New York

Originally published in French as *Le nom sur le mur*
in 2024 by Éditions Gallimard, Paris

Copyright © 2024 Éditions Gallimard
English translation copyright © 2025 Other Press

Production editor: Yvonne E. Cárdenas
Text designer: Julie Fry
This book was set in Galliard

10 9 8 7 6 5 4 3 2 1

Library of Congress Cataloging-in-Publication Data
Names: Le Tellier, Hervé, 1957– author | Hunter, Adriana
    translator
Title: The name on the wall / Hervé Le Tellier ; translated
    from the French by Adriana Hunter.
Other titles: Nom sur le mur. English
Description: New York : Other Press, 2025. | "Originally
    published in French as Le nom sur le mur in 2024
    by Éditions Gallimard, Paris" —Title page verso. |
    Includes bibliographical references.
Identifiers: LCCN 2025010336 (print) | LCCN 2025010337
    (ebook) | ISBN 9781635425451 paperback |
    ISBN 9781635425468 ebook
Subjects: LCSH: Chaix, André, 1924–1944—Fiction | World
    War, 1939–1945—Underground movements—France—
    Fiction | France—History—German occupation, 1940–
    1945—Fiction | LCGFT: Historical fiction
Classification: LCC PQ2672.E11455 E6613 2025 (print) |
    LCC PQ2672.E11455 (ebook) | DDC 843.914—dc23/
    eng/20250429
LC record available at https://lccn.loc.gov/2025010336
LC ebook record available at https://lccn.loc.gov/2025010337

PRAISE FOR *THE ANOMALY*

"[A] literary phenomenon...[*The Anomaly*] swerves between various genres—science fiction, a thriller, love stories, an introspective work—without being confined by any of them."
—*New York Times*

"*Manifest* meets *Lost* in *The Anomaly*...[a] puzzle box of a sci-fi thriller."
—*PopSugar*, Best New Mystery and Thriller Books of the Month

"Humorous, captivating, thoughtful—existentialism has never been so thrilling."
—*Kirkus Reviews* (starred review)

"A striking thought experiment...Le Tellier delivers some sharp social comedy here...But behind the comedy are more profound psychological questions about individual freedom...[*The Anomaly*] is priceless."
—*Times Literary Supplement*

"An extraordinary mix of existential thriller and speculative fiction...This thought-provoking literary work deserves a wide readership."
—*Publishers Weekly* (starred review)

When bad men combine, the good must associate;
else they will fall, one by one, an unpitied sacrifice
in a contemptible struggle.

EDMUND BURKE
Thoughts on the Cause of the Present Discontents

Perhaps revolutions are not the train ride, but
the human race grabbing for the emergency brake.

WALTER BENJAMIN
Preparatory notes for *On the Concept of History*

The Name on the Wall

A Childhood Home

I WAS LOOKING FOR a "childhood home," I'd explained to the real estate agent: not a vacation villa, not a "fixer-upper" ruin, not a "designer house," not a "quirky property," one of those sheepfolds or silkworm farms converted into a home where you knock your head on livestock-height doorframes.

No, I wanted a house where I could invent some roots for myself, and also a house in a living village, where you can do your shopping in the grocery store and have a drink at the café, in the Provençal part of the Drôme region, where I've had friends for a long time. So I visited this former coaching inn, ventured briefly into the small vegetable garden at the back, with its views across to the summits of the Miélandre and the Grand Ruy, and ascended the stone staircase to the bedrooms and a dusty attic. Of course, I'd found it; this was my childhood home. A solid, thick-walled two-story building a couple of hundred years old, in the heart of the hamlet of La Paillette in Montjoux, very close to Dieulefit.

Tina, the owner, was a ceramicist. She was also German. She'd lived there for nearly two decades until, at sixty-five, she felt the work was asking too much of her muscles and her back, and it was time she went to paint watercolors in Granville. Her work with clay channeled Nicolas de Staël dabbling in enamel, and a horizontal strip on the roadside façade of the house was covered with glazed ceramic plaques screwed to the wall at eye level. When she left, she took all but one of them with her. It was her gift and her mark, which I promised to preserve.

When the last plaque at the far right-hand end was removed, a name appeared, capital letters carved with a sharp point into the greige render: ANDRÉ CHAIX. On closer inspection, the R of ANDRÉ is a scaled-up lowercase letter. When we sit out having lunch in this courtyard in the cool shade of the big plane tree, we can hardly make out the letters. I doubt that the wall, which is bare stone in places, has ever been re-rendered. I got used to this name on the wall and eventually forgot about it.

I know a few people named Chaix. Particularly the novelist and translator Marie Chaix: she was the partner of Harry Mathews, the Oulipian writer and a great friend of Perec. But the name Chaix was that of her first husband, Jean-François, who was from the Savoie region, and she had kept it as her surname. Just like her elder sister Anne Sylvestre, she refused to bear her father Albert Beugras's name. Beugras, who'd been Doriot's right-hand man, had fled to Germany at the end of World War II, been imprisoned by the Americans and protected by their secret services. When they finally

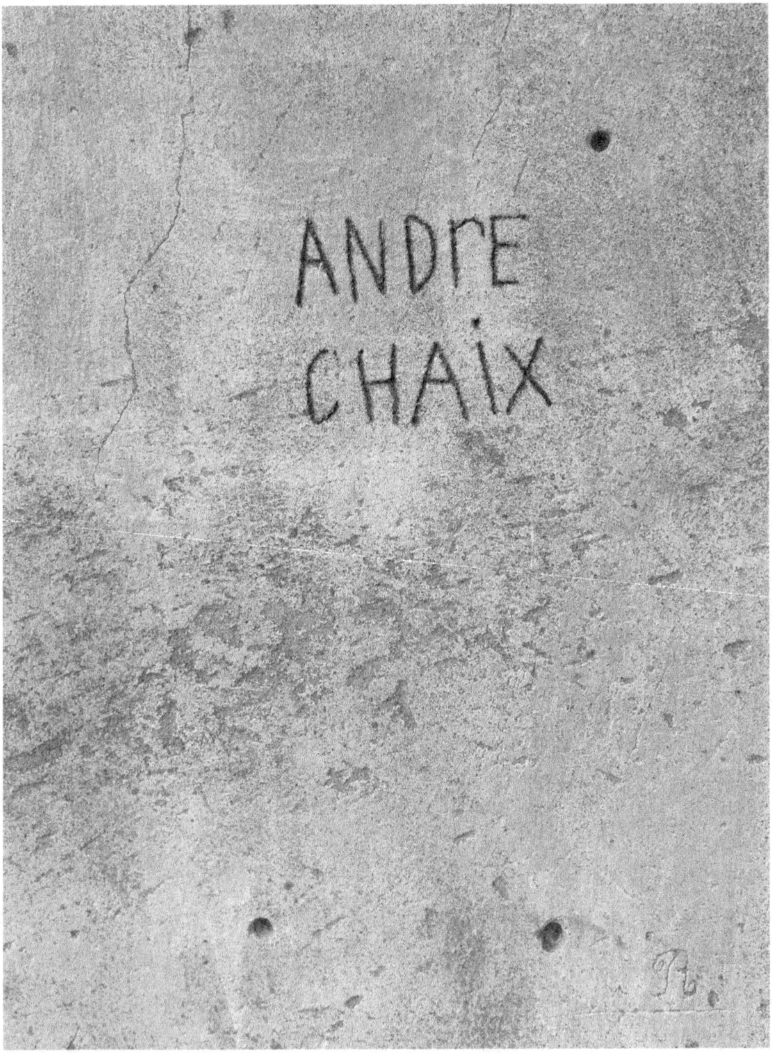
ANDrE
CHAiX

agreed to hand him over to the French authorities, Beugras narrowly escaped the death penalty. Marie describes all this in her novel *The Laurels of Lake Constance*, which was subtitled *Chronicle of a Collaboration* in the original French. That's a digression—the first of many—but its relevance will soon become clear.

This was early March 2020. A few friends and I had set up a writing residence at La Paillette when the threat of lockdown became a reality. We decided not to return to Paris in some instances or to Nantes in others, but to continue our work here. The page proofs of *The Anomaly* reached me thanks to a masked courier, virtual meetings proliferated, the expressions "face-to-face" and "in real life" took on new significance, and everyone made themselves fabric face masks. What was the point of going home?

On the small village square, next to the bakery and a few meters from my home, stands a monument "to the memory of the children of Montjoux who died for France." The wars were long ago, these deaths forgotten, and, in that strange spring of 2020 when time was suspended by the pandemic, I must have walked past the monument on twenty different mornings, laden with bread and croissants, indifferent and in a hurry. One day in, I think, May, a name caught my eye: CHAIX ANDRÉ (MAY 1924–AUGUST 1944). The dates said it all: Chaix had been in the Resistance, most likely the maquis, a young man with a short life, like so many others.

I didn't know anything about him, and several months went by before I saw him as the possible subject of a book.

I asked some questions, gathered fragments of collective memory, and learned something about who he'd been. A lot of the information in this inquiry was given to me by chance, almost by miracle, and I very soon knew I wanted to tell André Chaix's story. No doubt all lives are novelistic. Some more than others.

In his letters to Lucilius that explain the essence of Stoicism, Seneca describes someone at the bedside of an ailing man. Is he a friend who wants to be there in the final moments or a vulture with his eye on the dying man's estate? "The same act may be either shameful or honorable," Seneca replies. All that matters is the intention. I've examined my own. I'm not André Chaix's friend; in fact, would I have succeeded in being one, given that there's hardly anything to connect us?

Just a name on a wall.

I feel uncomfortable leaving that small phrase on a line by itself. A one-line paragraph is always a literary decision, sometimes an aestheticizing device, and I'm suddenly afraid that there's insincerity behind this stylistic effect, when the best style should ensure its own invisibility. Forgive me in advance if I come up with blundering sentences, inappropriate or affected turns of phrase, or metaphors that run aground in lyricism or pomposity. I've tried not to, even though I sometimes wanted to.

I haven't written a "novel," the "André novel." I haven't addressed him as if he were alive; I haven't chatted to him casually through the book as if he were a friend. That would have been an artificial exercise, and the artifice would have been inappropriate. True, I occasionally allowed my imagination to talk, but I would have found it obscene to invent, and I felt more comfortable traveling around this era that I didn't know but that was formative for me. I wanted to take you there and share with you the things I learned while I was writing. I also wanted the book to include images, photographs, so that André, his girlfriend, Simone, and a few others could have faces and bodies in your mind because they do in mine. Postcards and posters to conjure places and the period. If I had a recording of André's voice, I would publish it for people to hear.

Nor am I a historian, and yet this is very much History because André was one of its actors, heroes, and victims. I wasn't writing a dissertation, I didn't bury myself in secret archives, and I'd like to thank everyone who helped me find answers to my sometimes naive questions. In places I've used my own words to rephrase things I read in books and newspapers, heard in radio reports, or saw in documentaries. I may use too many quotes, but that's a way of appropriating, or not paraphrasing, other people's excellent formulations.

Forgive me also for the occasional mistakes, because of course there are some: memories can falter, accounts contradict one another. Please believe that, despite all this, I tried not to cheat.

The year 2024 is the centenary of André Chaix's birth and is eighty years since he died. But looking at the world as it is now, it seems obvious that we still need to talk about the Occupation, collaboration, fascism, racism, and othering to the point of complete destruction. So I didn't want this book to skirt around the monster against which André Chaix fought, I didn't want it to fail in giving a voice to the ideals for which he died, and I didn't want it to miss an opportunity to question our innermost nature, our need to belong to something greater than ourselves, which brings out the best and the worst in us.

I won't say that this book was an "obvious choice," an "obligation" or an "obsession." Franz Kafka told his friend Oskar Pollak that "a book must be the axe for the frozen sea inside of us." He's referring to reading more than writing. Let's just say that talking in simple terms about André Chaix became something I needed.

I can't find a way to think about death, my death; I can't tame the idea and finally give some meaning to a life that doesn't have one. I must have hoped that a respectful, honest, and circumspect book about this young man and what I think I know about him—and about myself—would be a milestone along this route.

CARTE D'IDENTITÉ

Nom *Chaix*
Prénoms *André*

Fils de *Chaix Jean*
et de *Sourbier Marcelle*
Profession *apprenti*
Nationalité *français*
Né le *23 mai 1924*
à *Montmeyran*
Département *Drôme*
Domicile *Montjoux*

SIGNALEMENT

TIMBRE
FISCAL
13
FRANCS

D.A
1,20
FRANC

TIMBRE FISCAL
40

TIMBRE FISCAL
40€

André Chaix

WRITERS OF OLD would breezily start their stories with the hero's birth. This method is as good as plenty of others that are now widely used. And yet we'll be starting with André's death, because that's why this book was born.

ANDRÉ PAUL CHAIX
Died for France on 08-23-1944
    (Dieulefit, 26—Drôme, France)
Status: soldier, Unit: French Forces of the Interior (FFI);
Born on 05-23-1924 in La Paillette Montjoux
    (26—Drôme, France)
20 years, 2 months, and 30 days
Source: Defense Historical Service, Caen
Classification: AC 21 P41118

That AC 21 P classification corresponds to the individual files of deportees and internees in the Resistance during World War II. It comprises 55,788 files. André Chaix is one of the 13,679 members of the FFI (French Forces of the Interior) killed during the course of the war. Two-thirds of them fell between June and September 1944.

A plaque on a wall in the chemin des Lièvres in Grignan tells us more:

On this site in Grignan on August 22, 1944
an F.T.P. [Francs-Tireurs et Partisans] detachment
of the 3rd Morvan battalion heading toward
Montélimar ran into a column of German
tanks. Seven young fighters were killed in this
engagement. The fighting at Nyons and Grignan
both received army commendations.

To those who pass this spot, remember.

A friend took the photograph for me. Yves lives very close to the chemin des Lièvres and had never noticed this. The plaque—well, this one, at least—doesn't name the Resistance fighters. You can't put everything on a plaque, it's true. Another plaque in town names Jean Barsamian, Aimé Benoît, André Chaix, Gabriel Deudier, Jean Gentili, and Robert Monnier. Two civilians were also killed: Paul Martin and Raoul Dydier. André was just one fighter among several, an "anonymous figure," as people sometimes say, but not a "nameless figure," because his name is carved into the marble of a monument in La Paillette.

The Drôme region's archives tell us that his father, Jean Chaix, was born in 1900 in Vesc, a village a few kilometers north of La Paillette, and his mother, Marcelle "née Sourbier," in 1903 in Montmeyran, to the southeast of Valence. The former died in 1983 and the latter ten years later. They lived forty and fifty years respectively grieving for a son.

Chaix is a common family name around Dieulefit. In fact, one in four of the five thousand people named Chaix in France lives in the Drôme. The final *x* is sometimes pronounced, as it is in Aix-en-Provence, and sometimes not, as in the French word for peace, *paix*, but in André's case it's pronounced subtly, without emphasis: *ādre ⬜ks*, then, like *mari ⬜ks* the writer. Chaix is the regional variant of the old Occitan word *cais*, "jaw," a nickname for a man with a prominent jaw, but in the Alps the word also means a variety of juniper used for making a syrup called chaï.

———

In the 1931 census, Jean Chaix is entered as a baker in La Paillette—the present-day bakery is still on the same site. It was in this building that he and Marcelle lived and worked. Shortly after the war, they would sell the lease, unable to stay on in the bakery that was haunted by memories of André. They had a second son, Marcel, four years André's junior. A sepia-toned photograph protected under glass and surrounded by an aluminum frame brings the two brothers together. They must be about eight and twelve; their hair is suitably neat and they're smiling at the photographer.

The fact that I was able to hold this photo in my hand is thanks to several people. In August 2023 an exhibition about the Resistance in the Drôme was held in Taulignan. The website mentioned the clash in Grignan, the brief combat during which André Chaix and several other maquisards lost their lives, and André's name was featured. I contacted the organizers and we arranged to meet at the community center. Between a US Army jeep and a reconstruction of life in the maquis complete with a crystal radio set broadcasting messages from Radio London, they handed me a small cardboard box, about the size of a postcard and one centimeter deep, held shut with a gray ribbon. Taped carelessly on it was a scrap of paper with just the word "André." The family had handed over everything that remained of a long-dead great-uncle to ensure that his memory wasn't completely lost. I immediately opened the box, and this frame—with André and his brother smiling out of it—appeared on top of various envelopes and photographs. As if ashamed of desecrating a tomb, I didn't dare delve further. I closed the box

carefully and waited till I was back in La Paillette to spread its contents over my desk.

It contained many things, all of them precious and so small: André's ID card; his certificate confirming that he was an apprentice at "Dieulefit Pottery"; the article in the *Dauphiné libéré* newspaper announcing his funeral at the cemetery in Montmeyran on October 12, 1949; a page from a book folded into four; a tract from the Francs-Tireurs et Partisans (an armed Resistance party set up by the French Communist Party); two envelopes containing letters that André had sent to his parents; a dozen photographs with notched edges, as was fashionable at the time; a small rusted metal box of laxative sweets called "Fructines-Vichy"—you couldn't make it up—"a sensible treatment for constipation and its consequences" (the product still exists, I don't know how effective it is); and a box filled with tiny photos, obviously contact sheets that André had cut up. There's also an embroidery in red thread with the letters *A* and *C* intertwined, a small brown leather billfold, and lastly, incongruously, a shockingly intimate and living thing—his cigarette holder.

I had these scraps of André Chaix's life before me. In one photo, the young man is standing, balancing on a horse's back; in another, he's skiing between the linden trees on the snowbound byroad toward Dieulefit on which my house stands; in another he's walking arm in arm with his fiancée. Her name is Simone, if I'm to believe the brief message of love that André wrote to her on the back of the snapshot. But I'll come to her later.

———

It's strange, but until then I'd never wanted, never dared, to picture André, his features, his build. To this day I don't try to imagine his voice or his accent. In these images from bygone days, André must be what? nineteen, but he looks a lot older. A maturity in his expression, an assurance in his bearing. He looks tall; he's athletic; his face is open, his eyes clear, and he has "quite the face" too. An actor's face, even. A touch of the young Jean Gabin, or Burt Lancaster, to choose people from his time, or Marlon Brando, who would also be celebrating his centenary in 2024. Marcelle must have been so proud of her firstborn.

An employer's record states that in April 1943 "Chaix André" became a "category 7" apprentice at the "ceramic works in Dieulefit." A document signed by the manager, André Le Blanc, on April 20, the day Hitler celebrated his fifty-fourth birthday. The apprentice André was only eighteen, fate could still tilt a hundred different ways, but this baker's son already wanted a different life, and he started by swapping an oven at 500 degrees for one at 2,200 degrees. The workshop was on rue du Savelas on the banks of the Jabron, a small river that runs through Dieulefit. André would come from place Chateauras on which the temple stood, would walk up the bustling rue du Bourg and turn left just after the church.

Montjoux's elementary school is moments from the bakery, opposite the coaching inn and the wall with the name engraved on it.

I wanted to find the young André's report cards, but a century—or nearly—later, it was too much to ask that the Department of Education had kept a single one. And if it had, I would have found this conservatism a little worrying. André's writing in letters and on the backs of photographs can look wobbly, but there aren't all that many mistakes, and the turn of phrase is often elaborate. And anyway, as the blotches testify, you try writing neatly with a Sergent-Major fountain pen!

Next to the bakery in La Paillette there's also what was then the village's only café-restaurant: the Café Ponson, run by Prosper... Ponson, of course. I found a photograph of it on an old postcard. André probably delivered croissants there in the morning and bread at lunchtime. Prosper left La Paillette for Montélimar shortly after the war, and since then half a dozen restaurateurs have successively run the café-restaurant.

5 — LA PAILLETTE - Place Léopold Mourier et entrée du Village

Lib. F. Baume - Montélimar

Twenty years, two months, and thirty days is the tally given by AC 21 P. Seven thousand three hundred ninety-seven days. I was born in April 1957, and on July 22, 1977, I was the age André was when he died — to the day. A haiku that is naive and profound in equal measure, as a haiku should be, tells us that we unwittingly celebrate the anniversary of our future death every year.

What can I have been up to on that Friday, July 22? France was "under Giscard," and I was probably getting ready for the antinuclear demonstration on the 30th against the Creys-Malville Superphénix reactor. It wasn't especially heroic, even if the prefect for the Isère region did threaten to open fire on the demonstrators, which he did with stun grenades; even if a thirty-year-old physics teacher, Vital Michalon, would die at the scene, his lungs ruptured, most likely due to a stun grenade—or, as per the investigator's version, a Molotov cocktail. And, most importantly, the woman I loved had died by suicide a few months earlier; she too had just turned twenty. Of course, dying at age twenty links André and Piette. But this link, objective though it may be, is tenuous. It occurred to me only after months of note-taking. There's nothing to prove I was in denial, which is popular psychology's inevitable argument: the patient must be obsessed with kangaroos, because he never talks about them. Let's say it's just an objective coincidence. Right now, as I type these words, that day in 1977 is further away than it was on August 23, 1944. The war was still so close, but I wasn't yet mature enough to be aware of the fact.

May 23, 1924, the day André was born, isn't too much of a historical blur for me. I now know that a future singer, Charles Aznavour, was born the day before. But I was aware that Lenin had died in January 1924 and that the Thirteenth

Congress of the Russian Communist Party was held from May 23 to 31 the same year. It's no exaggeration to say that André was born when the 1917 October Revolution died, given that at this congress Leon Trotsky's theories were deplored, and Stalin defended his project for "Socialism in one country" and began his assumption of power. In Germany, the Nazi Party, allied with the "pagans" in the racist *Völkisch* movement, sent some thirty deputies to the Reichstag with 6.6 percent of the vote. The pendulum of history was beginning a tragic swing.

What I can surmise about André's political opinions is based on so little, just a yellowed FTP tract that he kept on him. For many people the initials *FTP* are now most likely to mean the File Transfer Protocol, which allows us to share documents via the internet. But since 1942 the FTP, the Francs-Tireurs et Partisans, had been an umbrella term for three armed organizations associated with the French Communist Party: the Special Organization; the Bataillons de la Jeunesse (youth battalions); and the special troops in the FTP-MOI, where *MOI* stood for *main-d'œuvre immigrée* (immigrant workforce), and which included, among others, the Manouchian group. The FTP represented only part of the French internal Resistance force that eventually grouped together under the aegis of the French Forces of the Interior.

André didn't hold a "party" card. Or rather I should say: If he was a member, how to prove it? With the advent of the German occupation in 1940, the French Communist Party destroyed its own archives for understandable reasons. In any event, the communist affiliations of FTP maquis units were all relative. The Drôme has long been rural socialist rather than working-class communist territory. Even though the Communist Party made a breakthrough in the 1936 elections, the department sent two SFIO (French Section of the Workers' International) and two Radical Socialist representatives to the Assemblée. And Justin Jouve, the mayor of Dieulefit up until 1941, was a socialist.

Besides, the Resistance was far from a chemically pure entity. It was a nebula that would take a while to establish its core, if it ever did. Some fought German invaders, others Nazism, and together they fought the "Boche." This minimalist communal goal wove improbable connections among men and women who were as individual, as unique as an Armenian laborer and poet named Missak Manouchian; a communist academic and teacher, Lucie Aubrac; or an antisemitic, Maurras-supporting member of the King's Camelots, as was Jean Moulin's no less heroic secretary Daniel Cordier, who underwent a profound shift until, at the end of the war, he described himself as "almost communist."

It's so complex, so muddled even, that in order to navigate his way through the labyrinth of different elements in the Resistance, André kept a handout from the CNE (the National Writers' Committee), whose members included François Mauriac and Paul Éluard, alongside Jean-Paul Sartre.

The back of the leaflet is covered with scrawled signatures. Marcel, André's brother, was working on signing his name, trying to find a calligraphic identity. Signing an FTP

CE QU'IL FAUT SAVOIR

Le sens de certaines abréviations de certaines dénominations fréquemment employées n'étant pas très clair dans tous les esprits, le Comité National des Ecrivains croit utile, pour éviter la confusion, d'en donner l'explication :

F. T. P. F. est l'abréviation de **Francs-Tireurs et Partisans Français.**

F. N. est l'abréviation de **Front National** de lutte pour la libération et l'indépendance de la France.

Les Francs-Tireurs et Partisans, c'est-à-dire les F. T. P., forment l'armée du **Front National** ou F. N.

Le Front National est une des deux grandes organisations de la Résistance Française. Le F. N. comprend les hommes venus de tous les horizons, de l'extrême gauche à l'extrême droite, sans distinction de religion, de race ou de classe, pourvu qu'ils combattent les Boches.

Les **F. T. P.,** armée du F. N., constituent en fait une armée du type populaire.

A. S. est l'abréviation de Armée Secrète.

M. U. R. est l'abréviation de Mouvements Unis de la Résistance (comprenant les mouvements : "Libération, Combat, Franc-Tireur").

L'Armée Secrète, c'est-à-dire l'A. S., est l'armée des **Mouvements Unis de la Résistance,** c'est-à-dire des M. U. R.

Les **Mouvements Unis de la Résistance** sont l'autre grande organisation de la Résistance Française.

F. F. I. est l'abréviation de Forces Françaises de l'Intérieur.

Les Forces Françaises de l'Intérieur, les F. F. I., représentent l'ensemble des organisations armées englobant les F. T. P. et l'A. S. L'état-major des F. F. I. est composé des représentants de chacune de ces deux organisations. Ce sont ces représentants qui choisissent parmi eux leur chef. Ceci se fait à tous les échelons. Il n'y a F. F. I. qu'autant qu'il y a des représentants à la fois des F. T. P. et de l'A. S. ayant constitué un état-major commun.

Les Milices Patriotiques défendent activement sur place la ville, le village, l'entreprise, et où elles sont recrutées, elles peuvent et doivent se transformer en une levée en masse de toute la population contre l'ennemi.

C. N. R. est l'abréviation de **Conseil National de la Résistance.**

Le Conseil National de la Résistance est l'organisme qui, à Paris, groupe les représentants de toutes les organisations de Résistance. Il est l'autorité suprême de la Métropole et l'interprète du Gouvernement Provisoire de la République siégeant à Alger.

Le **Comité de Libération Nationale** est l'organisme du pouvoir civil. Il est composé des représentants de toutes les organisations de la Résistance adhérentes au C. N. R. qui, localement, peuvent être considérées comme une force active. Aux représentants des organisations se joignent les personnalités marquantes de la population.

Les Comités de Libération Nationale sont constitués à tous les échelons du pays : commune, canton, département, région.

Le Comité National des ECRIVAINS (C. N. E.)

document was unwise, but perhaps these experimentations date from after the Liberation?

The title of the leaflet summarizes it all:

WHAT YOU NEED TO KNOW

The meaning of frequently used abbreviations of various organizations' names are not clear in many people's minds, and, to avoid confusion, the National Writers' Committee thought it useful to provide explanations:

F.T.P.F. is the abbreviation of **Francs-Tireurs et Partisans Français**.

F.N. is the abbreviation of **Front National** [National Front] that strives for liberation and independence for France.

The Francs-Tireurs et Partisans, or F.T.P., constitute the army of the **National Front** or F.N.

The National Front is one of the major organizations in the French Resistance. The F.N. comprises men from all walks of life, from the far left to the far right, regardless of religion, race or class, so long as they fight the Boches.

The **F.T.P.**, the F.N.'s army, are to all intents and purposes a people's army.

A.S. is the abbreviation of **Armée Secrète** [Secret Army].

M.U.R. is the abbreviation of **Mouvements Unis de la Résistance** [Unified Resistance Movements] (including the movements: "Libération," "Combat," and "Franc-Tireur" [irregular soldiers]).

The Secret Army, or A.S., is the army of the **Unified Resistance Movements**, or M.U.R.

The Unified Resistance Movements are the other major organization in the French Resistance.

F.F.I. is the abbreviation for the **Forces Françaises de l'Intérieur** [French Forces of the Interior].

The **French Forces of the Interior**, or F.F.I., represent all armed organizations including the F.T.P. and the A.S. The F.F.I.'s general staff comprises representatives from both of these organizations. Between them, these representatives choose which of them is to be their leader. This process is carried out at every administrative level. There are only as many F.F.I. as there are representatives of both the F.T.P. and the A.S. once they have formed a joint general staff.

The Patriotic Militias actively defend towns, villages, and businesses on-site, and in the places where they have been recruited, they can and should evolve into mass uprisings of the entire population against the enemy.

C.N.R. is the abbreviation of **Conseil National de la Résistance** [National Council of the Resistance].

The **National Council of the Resistance** is the Paris-based organization that brings together representatives of all Resistance organizations. It is the supreme authority in mainland France and the mouthpiece of the Provisional Government of the French Republic sitting in Algiers.

The [French] **Committee of National Liberation** is the body representing civilian power. It comprises representatives from all Resistance organizations that are members of the C.N.R. that, on a local level, can be considered an active force. As well as representatives of these organizations, it comprises leading figures from the population.

Committees of National Liberation have been established at every administrative level in the country: communes, cantons, départements, and regions.

The National WRITERS' Committee (C.N.E.)

The Germans had an advantage in trying to grasp this diversity: they grouped it all under one term — *terrorist*. It's such a practical word that it's still used extensively today.

✝

I visited the cemetery in Montmeyran with its cypresses and yews towering over the Rhône Valley. Protected by a low stone wall, it contains more than 1,000 graves, but only 548 are inventoried, because plots weren't registered until 1950. André Chaix's name isn't on the register, and I spent a long time walking up and down the paths, dazzled by the sun, but didn't find his grave.

There are a few grassy plots, overrun with wild lavender, anonymous plots with no stone or cross, and it must have been in front of one of these that a handful of people gathered for the ceremony on October 12, 1949.

MONTMEYRAN. — Funeral for an FFI soldier who died for France. — The mayor of Montmeyran invites the town council, the firefighting corps, children from the town's schools, the association of combattants from the two world wars, the association of former prisoners of war, all local societies, and the entire population to attend the funeral of the FFI soldier Chaix André, who was killed by the Germans at Grignan on August 23, 1944. The ceremony will be held on Wednesday, October 12, 1949, at 4:30 p.m. at Montmeyran church.

André Chaix's body was being moved into the family vault. His friends from the maquis attended; his father and mother; his brother, Marcel, then age twenty-one; a few cousins, such as Huguette, who is now ninety-five and still lives in La Paillette; and perhaps also his former fiancée, Simone, who was by then married and had a three-year-old daughter. Little Christiane must have stayed in Dieulefit with her father, Lucien.

I stayed there a long time looking for his grave, until the autumn night engulfed everything. So I left, swearing to myself that I'd be back. But I didn't return to the cemetery, perhaps for fear that if I did find where he was laid to rest, I would bring his death to life.

André will be forever a man without a grave.

Simone Reynier, the Fiancée

First photo with you my darling who for me will always
be the sweet and pure Simone of my devotion you and I
will go through this life together and it may sometimes
be tough but nothing will come between us but death.

My gentle kisses

Your Dédé forever

ANDRÉ WROTE THESE WORDS across the back of the sepia
photograph in which he and Simone stand tenderly arm in
arm. The picture was inside the "André" box. I've reread
what he wrote many times. They're such solemn sentences
for a teenager. Or perhaps it's the other way around, perhaps
they're a teenager's light-as-air words but they've been crys-
tallized in tragedy for all time.

The photo isn't dated, but it's late spring, or perhaps
already summer. André and Simone are both eighteen
and they both seem very serious as they look into the lens.

Première photo avec
toi ma chérie qui
seras toujours pour
moi la douce et
pure Simone de mes
amours avec toi
nous parcourrons
la vie dure parfois
mais rien ne nous
séparera à part
la mort toujours Bonne
année ton Bébé
Con de toujours

They're posing for a friend who's holding the camera, Marcel or perhaps Louis, Simone's older brother.

André and Simone have recently met. It was most likely at one of those parties in the *bories*, where the young gathered to drink and dance. In the Drôme, *bories* doesn't mean farms, as it does in Provence, the Tarn region, and Ardèche: here it means cavities in the mountainside, some of them adapted into rooms for decanting clay, caves that nature or man has carved out of the crumbly sandstone known as *safre*.

Safre is a pretty word. In 1690, Furetière said this of it in his *Dictionnaire universel* (universal dictionary): "Some write it Zafre. It is a fossilized & metallic soil, clod or glebe of blueish color, tending toward gray-black, which is the magnesia or bismuth of lead, which in small quantities makes very clear glass, & in large quantities makes it very blue; hence its use in counterfeiting sapphires, which gave it the name safre; & potters upon reducing it to a powder, daub it on their works, the which are black in their raw state, & which are a very fine blue when they have been fired in the kiln."

In antiquity, sapphires and lapis lazuli were confused. The Persians thought that the night was colored with sapphire laid over the celestial vault. The Egyptians traveled to the hereafter wearing sapphire eye-of-Horus amulets. The Romans attributed aphrodisiac qualities to it, but they did also attribute these qualities to honey and anchovies. Potters were aware of all this, and André must have heard about it during his months of apprenticeship at the ceramic works in Dieulefit. Perhaps one night when he and Simone watched the stars twinkling across a lapis lazuli sky, they pondered these ancient legends.

Some time later, when I was rereading André's words—his "First photo with you my darling"—I realized that the photo belonged to Simone and that, because it was now in "my" box labeled "André," she must at some point have returned it to her fiancé's family, along with others and perhaps the letters André mentions. If I was right, then she'd relinquished all these photos because she no longer wanted to look at them; she no longer wanted to read those words that conjured a happy life to come. Too much grief, as well as too much guilt for having to live on. I understand. Years after Piette's death, I threw away the pictures I still had of her. All except one, I must admit, but I eventually lost it. I would have liked to entrust them to someone, but who? A friend? I didn't want to read in anyone's eyes that I was *the* young widower. Her parents? They might have thought I wanted to forget their daughter, when all I wanted was to "turn the page," a metaphor that implies life may be a book.

But I was wrong: Simone hadn't given everything to the Chaix parents. When I met her daughter, Christiane, she told me that Simone had entrusted a purple envelope to her, and thirty years after Simone's death, Christiane still kept it very respectfully. The purple of the paper has faded, but that envelope contains everything of André that Simone couldn't bring herself to throw away: A dozen photographs. There isn't a single letter. And yet in one of the letters he sent to his parents—almost all of which end with the same request: "Please say hello to Simone for me"—he mentions writing to her.

But no, not a single letter remains. I will only ever read what André wrote to his fiancée on the backs of photographs.

"To Simone whom I love madly"

"Madly" is underlined.

"I hope you'll be loved madly," said another André, whose name was Breton, in *Mad Love*. André is posing with his hands on his hips on a road, perhaps the one to La Paillette, by the bridge over the Lez, coming from Montjoux. His torso is still a boy's, but he's also a slim young man. Looking smart casual in a round-necked T-shirt, which had become fashionable in the thirties, darted pants, a belt with a silvery buckle, and formal shoes. If the image had been published in *L'Illustration*, I would have believed a caption that read:

"The young Prince Gustaf of Sweden in casual attire, on summer vacation at his family's villa in Provence."

Never trust a snapshot or a cliché...they're even the same word in French.

And then there they both are, sitting on the edge of a well. André writes:

> At this well, I remade the wish that I've often whispered
> in your ear, and I'm sending you my loving kisses from
> my burning lips.
>
> Your fiancé Dédé

Of course, we can guess what André wished for: a happy life with Simone. Because, as he said himself, "nothing will come between us but death." We should always *wish* that we'll be happy, rather than swearing that we will be. Put the blame on fate if it so rarely keeps its promises. Put the blame on language if engaged couples are said to be each other's "intended."

Simone is less photogenic than André, but perhaps she just didn't much like photographs. A series of other pictures, in which she's next to André and surrounded by girlfriends on an outing to Montélimar, does her much more justice. Her daughter describes her as a tender and intelligent woman with a gentle face, a rare gift for patience, and great kindness; so much so that, without a shred of irony, she was nicknamed "Saint Simone."

Also in the purple envelope is this flowery card with the handwritten words "May happiness go through life with

you." It's a card they were sent for their engagement. At least, so I believe. Why else would she have kept it?

I got "engaged" to Piette—or rather she got engaged to me—in her still-dark bedroom at dawn on the first day of spring in 1977. She woke me to improvise a farcical ceremony, a secret and tender pastiche. She'd put an embroidered doily over her black hair, and a red and white checkered napkin over her hands. I had to quietly repeat after her: "I will love Piette even when she's very, very, very old and very, very ugly," "I will read Piette to sleep every night with *The Odyssey*," "There will always be *chouquettes* pastries in the house for Piette," and another thirty vows. I was moved, and terrified too, because I could tell how much even these eccentricities were committing me forever.

Over the next few years, I felt more comfortable filing other people's engagements in the "bygone world" department. A friend who had faith in my ability to make mischievous comments had even asked me to write a speech for his engagement. I surmised that engagements mostly came to a happy conclusion, but, alas, the two parties sometimes ended up marrying.

And yet no glimmer of irony comes to mind when I think of André and Simone's. They solemnly did what Piette had transformed into a parody, but there were elements of wonder, tragedy, and gravitas in theirs just as there were in ours, and I have absolutely no regrets about my pasteboard engagement.

There is, however, one sentence on the back of a photograph that shows that the future was fragile, because Simone was worrying about it and André needed to reassure her:

Under this mulberry tree I renewed the wish with my protector that whatever may happen to me, I should die remembering that you were my wife and not a passing girlfriend, as you always believed I wanted you to be.

Darling, believe me when I say I truly love you to distraction.

Simone had her doubts about how genuine André's commitment was. I liked this young woman's caution, the way she managed to be affectionately wary of her André. Time could have eventually proved her right; who's to know? They were only young, and the fates are capricious. Oscar Wilde said something along the lines that young men want to be faithful but aren't, while the old want to be unfaithful but can't.

But death ensured that Simone would never be a "passing girlfriend." André would be twenty years old forever, and Simone would always be his "wife."

On the back of another photo that shows them leaning against a wall, smiling, Simone wrote: "Look closely at André and you'll understand."

She was saying this to the whole world.

I would wager that the teenage Simone wrote these words as soon as she received the print, and to her they mean: "Look who this man is, see why I love him." A sentence full of admiration, pride, and joy. We must always admire the people we love. It's so admirable that we love them in the first place.

There are other possibilities, but I don't want to believe that Simone wrote this after André died, that these were dark words explaining why nothing and no one would ever console her. A miserabilist interpretation when everything points to the fact that, gentle though Simone was, she was a strong woman whose life had already been tough and arduous, and would continue to be so. She was the fourth child and the only daughter in a family with five children. Her

Regarder
bien André
il vous comprendrez

parents had divorced when she was eleven. At fourteen she'd been sent to board at the Le Gué convent in Le Poët-Laval only a few kilometers away. She'd spent two years of her schooling there, and then returned to live with her mother in Dieulefit. She wanted to be a teacher, but that meant years of studying to qualify and she couldn't afford it.

In 1943 and 1944, Simone was employed at the "chateaux," the mansions along the allée des Promenades. Later, she worked at the Moret draperies factory, then from home, where she finished the selvage on pieces of tweed and Prince of Wales check. Next, she moved to the Luffra shoe factory, which, like almost all of Dieulefit's small manufacturing businesses, has subsequently closed down.

If Queneau was right and history is the study of mankind's misfortune, then Simone has her rightful place in it, and this book could be dedicated to her. Before seizing this young woman's fiancé, the war had first robbed her of her father.

Célestin Reynier was what people call a character. He was born in Rochebaudin, a village to the north of Dieulefit, under the tall escarpments at Serre Gros. He worked on the family farm, and, in 1914, only weeks before he went off to war—the one that was meant to end all wars—the twenty-five-year-old Célestin married Solange. He was one of those men showered with machine-gun fire, cannon fodder, like all the peasant farmers who, out of some barrack-room logic, were lumped into the infantry. He went from one regiment to another, and on September 28, 1915, during the second offensive in the Champagne region, his unit was decimated and he was seriously injured.

That same day, only a few kilometers away, another soldier, the legionnaire Blaise Cendrars, was mutilated. In his autobiography, *The Bloody Hand*, Cendrars found a way to describe the butchery: "God is absent on the battlefield, and those who died at the beginning of the war, the poor little chicks in their madder red pants forgotten on the grass, left as many marks as—and were no more important than—so many cowpats in a meadow."

The foot soldier Célestin Reynier didn't die in his "madder red" pants—"They call me Madder, it's the name of a flower," the actress and singer Arletty would say in *Children of Paradise*—but the army brought him home from the front disabled, and pinned a Croix de Guerre with a bronze star to his uniform.

When he returned to the Dieulefitois area, Célestin was reunited with Solange. He more or less completely stopped working in the fields. Their children came along, and he became an itinerant distiller, going from houses to farms, from Poët-Laval to Taulignan and Valréas, transforming fruit harvests into spirits. But Célestin couldn't keep the still at arm's length; nor could his marriage withstand his way of life. In 1935, he and Solange divorced.

Eight years later, Célestin was drinking less—a case of *Résistance oblige*. He too had enrolled in the FTP, in Grignan. He may have been André's entry point into the maquis, but it's fair to say there were plenty of other possible candidates. Like many of the partisans, he was convinced that the Normandy landings on June 6 would be swiftly followed by others in the south, most likely in Marseille, Toulon, or Cannes, and this would catch the Reich's army in a pincer action. And so, on June 8, following instructions from Radio London—whose primary objective was to keep the Germans where they were all over the country—the FTP and Resistance fighters in the Gaullist Armée Secrète (Secret Army) joined forces to enter Valréas and occupy strategic positions in the town. The French police retreated to their barracks, anxious of reprisals now that the war appeared to be lost for Germany and the Vichy regime. "To obey is to betray," the slogan of the Resistance, was daubed in white paint on the wall outside their shack. In the end, they laid down their weapons and came out with their arms up: they weren't harmed in any way. Valréas jubilantly celebrated the maquisards' intervention, but the town was isolated, even though another site, the city of Annonay on the far side of the Rhône, was also liberated for a few days.

The Germans had spies, agents who had infiltrated the maquis. One of these agents, René Claude, alias Roger Ferrand, reported the positions held by the Resistance, and, just two days later, a pair of the Luftwaffe's Stuka fighter jets machine-gunned them. On June 12 there was a German counterattack by the 5th Company, known as the "Brandenburg Company," and the 9th "Hohenstaufen" Armored Division of the Waffen-SS. They numbered more than one thousand, all of them in vehicles, with heavy tanks and armored cars. There were fewer than two hundred maquisards, and they were ill equipped with only six light machine guns and some pistols, mostly confiscated from the police. Colonel Achiary, the maquis' commanding officer, gave orders to retreat, but the order didn't reach entrenched FTP men, because it was intercepted by an infiltrator. So the FTP held their positions around Taulignan, and Célestin Reynier, a member of the "Guion group," occupied a small trench to the south of the village by the road to Valréas.

History books and commemorative monuments are there to tell the rest of the story. The Hohenstaufen Armored Division entered Valréas, followed by the Brandenburg Company. Wehrmacht soldiers machine-gunned through the streets, firing at doors and windows; they set fire to a few buildings, looted houses, and stole food, jewelry if they found it, and even bicycles. It was an unequal fight; the few partisans who couldn't escape were captured and some of them killed on the spot. The mayor of Valréas, Jules Niel, was ordered to gather the inhabitants on the town square. At five in the afternoon, Major Unger harangued the assembled population, then walked off to his headquarters, the hôtel Thomassin, which was very nearby. An officer gave the order for the twenty-seven captured maquisards to be lined up in front of the wall of the printworks, along with some thirty hostages taken at random from the small, corralled crowd. Then the firing squad began its slow carnage. The soldiers shot their prisoners in batches of five, stopping between salvos for a drink at the hôtel Thomassin across the street, continuing like this till they were drunk. Before collapsing under gunfire, some prisoners called out the name of a loved one; others sang the first bars of "La Marseillaise" or the "Internationale."

More than fifty bodies lay on the sidewalk. Blood flowed along the little drainage channel, a stream of scarlet on dry earth. The officer forbade anyone to touch the bodies, but come nightfall, volunteers, firemen, and nurses went over to examine them. Five men were still breathing. Four would survive their wounds.

Farther north, fifty motorized German soldiers retook the village of Taulignan. It was defended by only twenty to thirty maquisards, among them Célestin Reynier. With no order to retreat, they didn't give up. It was a punitive expedition, and seven inhabitants were shot straightaway. Célestin was captured in his "trench" along with four of his fellow fighters. They were taken to Montluc prison in Lyon, where they were tortured for five days. Around noon on June 18, he was hauled from his cell, shackled, and loaded into a military truck with about twenty others. A militia-owned Citroën Traction led the way as they headed past Bron and Saint-Priest toward the Isère.

Célestin and his comrades can have been in no doubt about their final destination. One feature of death is that it is unthinkable, so what that feels like—to be trundling toward it, to think about the remaining time in that noise and heat and half light—I can't imagine. In Jean-Pierre Melville's film *Army of Shadows*, Philippe Gerbier, the Resistance fighter played by Lino Ventura, gives a voice-over as his character walks down the prison's long corridor on the way to the firing squad: "It's impossible not to be afraid when you're going to die. It's because I'm too blinkered, too much of an animal to believe it will happen. But if I don't believe it right up to the last moment, right up to the narrowest borderline, then I'll never die."

After an interminable hour, the small convoy reached the village of Roche and stopped, and the truck reversed into a field of oats still in flower. The twenty men were bundled out, they walked a few paces into the long grass, and the German soldiers shot them—two bullets in the back of the neck or the temple—and abandoned their bodies there.

During Klaus Barbie's trial in 1987, these war crimes would be remembered among the huge number of charges. And it is no coincidence that Barbie was imprisoned in Montluc throughout the trial.

The inhabitants of Roche found twenty bodies. Three of them were identified, and a few days later the seventeen others were buried in a common grave once they had been inventoried and photographed: Simone's father's coffin bears the number 8. Célestin Reynier would be the last to be named, on September 7, 1945. He was identified "from a photograph" by his eldest son, Louis. For a year his children and friends had lived in hope. Perhaps he'd been deported; perhaps he would come home from Buchenwald or Dachau?

I can imagine the cataclysm Simone experienced with her father vanishing into the French prison system, then losing her fiancé two months later; I understand that—confronted with life's betrayal—she refused to give up; and I understand just as readily the circumstances of her marriage barely two years later to Lucien, Lucien Jouve. Her little Christiane was born not long afterward, in late 1946. Simone would soon tell Christiane about her grandfather and, later, when the child was old enough to understand, about André. Cendrars, again: "Live, oh! Go ahead and live, regardless of what comes next! Feel no remorse. You're not the judge."

For those who love an epilogue or are simply interested to know whether the culprits of the Valréas massacre would be punished, let's say it straight out: no. There was certainly a trial, in February 1951, a military hearing. But each of the officers recorded as having attended in person—from Major Unger to Commandant Hentsch—shifted the blame onto someone else. An exonerated German lieutenant, Gerhard

Blanck, who was in command of the Hohenstaufen Armored Division, testified that the sleeve of the lieutenant in charge of the firing squad had "oak leaves" on it—the emblem of the Brandenburg Company. This detail identifies the commander of the French legionaries, and fanatical Nazi, Lieutenant Helmut Demetrio. Of the four suspects, Demetrio would eventually be the only one to stand trial, but because Blanck was not called as a witness, he was acquitted. Two months later, in April 1951, Demetrio was tried for a similar massacre by another military court, this time in Bordeaux. He was sentenced to ten years imprisonment, he served only two, and that was that: he was back in Karlsruhe, where he taught music to schoolchildren and drank beer with old friends in white shirts and lederhosen.

In any event, after the amnesty law of August 6, 1953, regarding crimes or actions involving collaboration, French prisons no longer held a single person sentenced for offenses relating to the occupation. Even the murderers from Tulle, Figeac, and Argenton-sur-Creuse, the massacring culprits of Oradour-sur-Glane, and many others. Of the rare few who were imprisoned, all of them, absolutely all of them, were released in 1953. No one wanted to imprison the Malgré-Nous in Alsace, forcibly enlisted into the SS Das Reich 2nd Division, even though they represented two-thirds of the accused. The damning verdict of that military trial in Bordeaux would come to nothing, and when church bells in Alsace sounded the alarm after the sentences were announced, the amnesty came along and canceled them out. Sure, the poor, rural Creuse region could mourn its dead. It would have to yield to wealthy, industrial Alsace, the only region in France where no one had ever been a Nazi.

It would be wrong to think that lots of people slipped through the net. There was no net now because no one wanted there to be one. The United States, preoccupied with its Cold War against the Soviets, was setting up Operation Paperclip, which involved exfiltrating and recycling former Nazis who, it's true, were a bit excessive with their antisemitism but were also top-notch anti-communists.

I remember an episode of the cult French TV series *Dossiers de l'écran* that screened *And England Will Be Destroyed*, an East German spy film in which Resistance fighters tried to sabotage the launch of V-2 rockets. There was always a discussion after the film, and, in April 1973, that was where I first saw François Le Lionnais, of course not realizing that he was the founder and first president of the Oulipo literary movement. "FLL"—those were his Oulipian initials—was there as a former deportee to Camp Dora, a concentration camp where twenty thousand prisoners died, one-third of all the inmates; and where the V-1s and V-2s that were dropped on London were made. He had very clear memories of a deputy director who was a rocket expert and liked to attend hangings, when he wasn't busy deciding who should be hanged. The man's name was Wernher von Braun. He was seized upon by the Americans and traded his knowledge for immunity, right up to directing NASA for decades. He had declined the TV network's invitation to join the discussion. "My schedule," he'd replied. Le Lionnais was sure that was why . . .

In France there was a mood of reconciliation, a myth that the nation had been, if not resistant, at least united behind its Resistance. Article 45 of the Amnesty Law of August 1953 forbids even referring to the crimes committed. Nothing had happened. The president of the council, René Mayer, summed it up frankly: "National unity [is] above any pain, and still more urgent than any reparation."

Which is why, for a period of twenty years, not one official was invited to Oradour-sur-Glane by the town's Association Nationale des Familles des Martyrs (national association of martyrs' families). And when the time came to build the ossuary where the remains of the 643 assassinated victims would be laid to rest, the association refused any funding from the French state.

So Nazism, Then

THE LAW OF LARGE NUMBERS leaves no room for doubt, and I searched for a German soldier born, like André Chaix, on May 23, 1944, and who, like him, would live for twenty years, two months, and thirty days and die on August 23.

The central German federal database (file B 563-1 Kartei) alone lists nearly 2,200 soldiers born on May 23, 1924, who died at the front. It's not possible to run a combined search with the dates of death. But five million German soldiers died in the conflict, and in the course of just August 1944, the most murderous month of the whole war, nearly 450,000 perished or were reported missing. So it can be stated without too much room for error that on August 23, 1944, four or five German soldiers born on May 23, 1924, fell, five young men with short lives that paralleled André's. Of course there are others, from other nations, some of them even more numerous: Russians, the so often forgotten Chinese, and the Jews and Romani killed at Auschwitz, an extermination camp that was still "working" at the time. But we're not drawing up a balance sheet.

These twenty-year-old soldiers died in France, near Paris or Montélimar, at a time when the German Army was retreating in the face of advances from American, British, and French troops... It's even more likely that they fell near Krakow, Odessa, and Minsk, because the Eastern Front was such a bloodbath. On August 25, 1944, the day Leclerc's 2nd Armored Division entered a liberated Paris, the Red Army crossed the Vistula and advanced into Greater Germanic Reich territory.

Of those five Germans who died for Hitler, because of him, I know nothing; not their names nor their faces. Summoning them up, even this scantly, and talking of "parallel" lives, doesn't make them companions in misery confronting a nebulous common enemy by the name of Nazism, an indistinct and despicable monster of which they too were innocent victims. There is also such a thing as a guilty victim. Those young men *were* Nazism. If they hadn't been there to bear its arms and, in some cases, to perpetrate its crimes, in a word to incarnate it, then André Chaix would one day have turned twenty-one. And, you never know, a hundred.

But I do know this about them: they were nine years old when Hitler took power, and all of them joined the Hitler Youth, at the very latest on the day they turned fifteen. They had no choice. They were all mobilized in the Wehrmacht in May 1942, at the age of eighteen. Here too they had no choice. One of them, being more fanatic than the others, may have decided to join the Waffen-SS, Himmler's

"German elite." After all, even Günter Grass, the writer and figure of German rectitude in the postwar years, was enlisted in it in the final months of the war, and for boys of the time there was "nothing frightening about Waffen-SS officers." None of us is very sensible at seventeen.

They were told a thousand times: they belonged to the Aryan race, the superhuman race, the Übermensch, and they were in absolutely no doubt about its superiority. And even if Germany had been suffering setback upon setback for months, perhaps they continued to have faith in Nazi propaganda and died still confident of the Reich's ultimate victory.

I don't know whether clemency is my forte. But I've seen dozens of them framed in black, the serious faces of young German soldiers in announcements like this one that reads:

Du warst so gut, Du starbst zu früh,
Wer Dich gekannt, vergißt Dich nie.

Du warst so gut, Du starbst zu früh,
Wer Dich gekannt, vergißt Dich nie.

You were so good, you died too soon,
None who knew you will forget you.

And I feel pity for Emmerich Blaschko, who was born on November 3, 1925, and died on October 22, 1944, in Bassing in the Moselle region. This nineteen-year-old corporal was enlisted in the 11th Panzer Division that had fatally wounded André Chaix two months earlier. Pity too for many of the young men swallowed up by the black spiral of the swastika. But I can find no shred of indulgence for the people, in France and other countries, who allowed their hatred or—worse—their cowardice or careerism to define their destiny.

With their actions and intentions, André and Célestin certainly chose theirs. A twenty-year-old Simone wept for the two most important men in her life, her father and her fiancé, two free men. Sartre was right to define freedom with these apparently very provocative words: "Never were we freer than under the German occupation...The more the Nazi venom crept into our thoughts the more each precise thought became a conquest."

When an event upends our whole existence, it's often only years later that we can evaluate it. I was ejected from childhood by a movie, Alain Resnais's *Night and Fog*, which I watched at the high school ciné-club. Those images of heaped bodies being tumbled into ditches by bulldozers abruptly debarred me from a carefree life. I was twelve years old and was reduced to questions and anger. I found some answers. The anger, fury even, never abated. It's good that it has remained intact.

Nazism is not a page like any other in the history of humankind. All the better if it's impossible to discuss it serenely, and serene this chapter won't be. All the better if baptizing a little boy Adolf has become a subject of dark comedy. All the better if the unfairly denigrated Godwin's Law invalidates all abusive generalizations and confirms that—sorry to break the bad news—painting watercolors, being a vegetarian, or loving dogs proves absolutely nothing.

The chronology of Adolf Hitler's rise to power remains an object lesson. Let's make it brief: Hindenburg appointed him chancellor in late January 1933, a month later the Reichstag was burned down, Hitler blamed the communists and had their leaders arrested, and in the elections on March 5, bolstered by the restrictive decree "regarding the Reichstag fire," his party, the NSDAP, secured 43.9 percent of the vote and his nationalist allies 8 percent. Four days later the Nazis seized the Länder that they did not yet control. On March 21, the first concentration camp opened in Dachau. On the 23rd, Hitler gained total power, and on April 1, he ordered a boycott of Jewish stores throughout Germany. Then the race toward war began, and no one in Europe could pretend they were unaware of it.

Barely nine weeks separate Hitler's accession to the chancellery from dictatorship and the first antisemitic measures. A point to remember: fascist regimes operate faster than any democracy.

The Third Reich was supposed to last a thousand years; it would manage twelve. But those twelve years were enough to mold some terrifying men and women. Nazism catalyzed an extraordinary aptitude for inhumanity present in some specimens of humanity. It endlessly asks us the question, what is a man and what shapes him?

"Ordinary people do not know that everything is possible," said David Rousset, a survivor of the Buchenwald concentration camp. But do they know what they're capable of?

This small ad appeared in a Berlin newspaper dated 1944:

"Working women in good health, ages 20 to 40, sought for a military site."

Hundreds of young women from poor families and with no qualifications replied. What were they promised? A decent salary, free meals, accommodation, and clean clothes. The clothes were SS uniforms; the military site doing the recruiting, Ravensbrück concentration camp. It is about eighty kilometers north of Berlin and was intended primarily for women and children: Jews, lesbians, communists, the homeless, and objectors. Thirty thousand would die there, of hunger, disease, and exhaustion; some were gassed, others hanged.

On discovering what their work would entail, a few young recruits immediately resigned. No one would hold it against them and their defection would have no consequences for them or their families. The others, the overwhelming majority, proudly joined the SS. They would prove to be sadistic and merciless torturers. Ordinary women committing atrocities that won't be described here precisely because of their atrocity. One of them, Irma Grese, was promoted to Auschwitz and then Bergen-Belsen, and earned the nicknames the "Hyena of Auschwitz" and the "Beast of Belsen." And yet she'd been raised in an atmosphere so devoid of hatred that when her anti-Nazi father heard which post she'd accepted in 1942, he said he never wanted to see her again. Of the thousands of female SS guards who worked at Ravensbrück, sixty-seven would be tried and very few convicted. Irma Grese was tried and hanged.

An American historian, Christopher Browning, published a book some thirty years ago called *Ordinary Men* and subtitled *Reserve Police Battalion 101 and the Final Solution in Poland.* This battalion of some five hundred men was recruited from the police force, so they were specifically Germans who wanted to escape the Wehrmacht and the war. With an average age of about forty, they hadn't fought in World War I, came from "Red Hamburg," and had grown up well before Nazi indoctrination. In fact, this battalion that was attached to the SS comprised few members of the Nazi Party. These individuals, despite being the least susceptible to adhere to Nazi theses, would shoot dead thirty-eight thousand Jews—men, women, and children—and deport forty-five thousand.

The terrible thing about numbers is that, beyond a certain point, they don't mean anything to us. The philosopher Günther Anders calls this the "supra-liminal," something that is too big to be understood. Let's say that it takes more than a day and a night to read out loud the names of every victim of the 101st Battalion.

What Christopher Browning demonstrates is that submitting to authority, peer pressure, and a "sense of duty" can churn out killers with no qualms. These men weren't psychopaths or monsters but "ordinary men" happy to celebrate Christmas with a drink after a day of slaughter.

Browning's book went more or less unnoticed. But in 1996, a young Harvard professor of political science revisited the example of this battalion and adapted his thesis for a general readership, publishing it as *Hitler's Willing Executioners.* He states that, of all nations, the Germans alone had wanted to "eliminate" Jews since the early 1800s; and, having brought Hitler to power, that is exactly what they did. This book by Daniel Goldhagen, who is incidentally an eloquent and telegenic writer, struck a chord with a wide readership. Better than that—it petrified them: the first-person accounts of very commonplace, terrifyingly cruel Germans utterly convinced his readers. Surely, Goldhagen was right: the Germans of the 1930s and 40s really were devils in uniform. By putting these testimonies and their ideology center stage, the book made the overly complex work of Browning and all other historians look bland. The unnuanced simplicity of his depiction appealed to many people, and to me too, I admit. Everyone wanted easily identifiable culprits: young Germans in the late twentieth century could point the finger at their grandparents, and Europeans could glibly exonerate themselves from all their forebears' collaborations.

It would be nice if it were that simple. It was not: the best historians, from Raul Hilberg to Ian Kershaw, criticized Goldhagen's simplistic approach, found fault with him for referring mostly to incriminating documents, for being biased in his choice of legal sources, and for unfairly generalizing his preconceptions. Goldhagen was also forgetting that, when confronted with the persecution of Jews, other members of German society had not been entirely passive, despite their own terror. It's hard to tell what Germans thought of this insane annihilation. At the start of the war, Victor Klemperer, the Jewish writer who owed his survival to his status as the husband of an "Aryan," wondered in his diary: "Who can judge the mood of eighty million people, with the press bound and everyone afraid of opening their mouth?"

As for the premise that the Germans were, exceptionally among all nations, ontologically antisemitic, that is also open to discussion: as soon as the occupiers had opened the floodgates to barbarity, the Latvians, Lithuanians, Ukrainians, Poles, and plenty more besides proved no less savage or zealous. In France, when the Nazis gave orders to deport Jews but to spare "descendants of Jews born in France or naturalized before 1860," it was Pétain—but why do we need to keep repeating the fact?—who struck through this clause with his own hand and sent tens of thousands of French Jews to Nazi abattoirs. And then there was the French police force itself, which didn't seem overly reticent—litotes, of course—to obey Pétain's orders.

Apologies for reiterating the fact, but *dégueulasserie*, despicableness, knows no boundaries. "What is *dégueulasse*?" asked Jean Seberg.

There's no appetite in these pages to showcase a whole Célinery of *Trifles for a Massacre*, an ignominious parade of Rebatet's *Décombres* (wreckage), one of those logorrheic outpourings gleaming with antisemitic loathing and produced by writers who are well known to be French, well established, and well read. It's a reliable way to debase yourself, spending time with these people's worst writings and marveling at the audacity of the criminal excesses—and I am guilty of succumbing to this. Everything has already been said about a certain Céline who clamored for so much Jewish blood that he sickened even Otto Abetz, the Reich's ambassador in France. I mean, they're like characters from a book! Look at Céline, the cursed exile! Rebatet, the dandy who survived a death sentence! Brasillach, the enfant terrible who was shot to serve as an example! Oh, madam, such devilish style, such rich, soaring prose, sir! Reading about the "little Yids," the "flea-ridden rabble," the "fucking Jews," and all those swarming exclamation points...and ellipses...such genius! How not to shudder with literary ecstasy? How fail to have esthetic convulsions? That's the question I'm asking you! When the respectable German bourgeoisie played host to Hitler with all their porcelain and crystal, they too had the vapors to think that under his tailcoat this hoodlum was carrying a pistol . . .

We haven't gone off-topic here. Of course, I'm prepared to bet, André Chaix hadn't read their pamphlets recruiting people to the slaughter, had never opened *Le Pilori* (the pillory) or *Je suis partout* (I am everywhere), antisemitic newspapers that had plenty of subscribers in Dieulefit. But this momentary exasperation with those who sowed hatred doesn't distance us from him. Quite the opposite. It is against them too that he fought, and because of people like them that he died at age twenty.

You could watch the Nuremberg trials ten times, and you would be stunned ten times by those pleas of "*nicht schuldig*," those "not guiltys" from individuals still dripping with blood, from the multi-minister Hermann Goering to Alfred Rosenberg, responsible for Germany's "Eastern Territories."

But the feeling of belonging to a *Volk*—a "people," a "race"—was powerful. It was easy to poke fun at the Nazis by saying Aryans were "as blond as Hitler, as tall as Goebbels, and as slender as Goering," but racism, which went hand in hand with colonialism, had already impregnated every European society, and perhaps German society more than any other. France had had its Dreyfus Affair, its Maurras, its Céline, but Germany had its Richard Wagner, whose work contributed to the establishment of a "German narrative" and who wanted to "de-Jew" European culture as early as 1850. Hitler draws much inspiration from him in *Mein Kampf.* And between 1904 and 1908, the kaiser's Germany initiated the twentieth century's first genocide—against Namibia's Herero and Nama.

The Nazis need to be taken seriously, and so do their delusions. The Nazi view was that the history of humanity was in fact a history of biological combat between races. With the advent of national socialism, the superior Indo-Germanic race was rebelling at last, having always been the victim of enemies who wanted to eradicate it—from the Persians to the Romans, right up to these Gallo-Roman commoners, the "female race" crossbred with Jews and Blacks that drove the French Revolution, sullied by its egalitarian ideas. The Nazi project could only ever be a total victory. Besides, once the Germans had triumphed, the SS Race and Settlement Main Office had plans beyond exterminating the Jews: enslaving and sterilizing the Slavs, and then all other inferior races. Nazism was initially a fight for Good that became confused with racial purity, a fight conducted by very human beings against others who were barely human at all. The murders were a chore, sometimes unpleasant, but necessary. An *Aufgabe*.

When the war was definitively over, the fact that Hitler and Goebbels took their own lives in their bunkers was not due to fear of being tried nor shame for any crime; it was because the Germanic race would now be extinguished. So they might as well die. Which is also why Magda Goebbels dressed her six children in white and poisoned them with cyanide, feeling no remorse because she was sparing them a life in the monstrous world of subhumans that now loomed, a world in which Jews, Slavs, and Negroes would have triumphed.

So, there were Aryans and there were inferior races, headed up by the Jewish race. When the doctor of chemistry Primo Levi first met his boss, Doktor Ingenieur Pannwitz, in Monowitz, an industrial annex to Auschwitz where Pannwitz was developing synthetic fuels, he saw something in his eyes that wasn't even contempt:

> Because that look was not one between two men; and if I had known how completely to explain the nature of that look, which came as if across the glass window of an aquarium between two beings who live in different worlds, I would also have explained the essence of the great insanity of the third Germany.
>
> One felt in that moment, in an immediate manner, what we all thought and said of the Germans. The brain which governed those blue eyes and those manicured hands said: "This something in front of me belongs to a species which it is obviously opportune to suppress. In this particular case, one has to first make sure that it does not contain some utilizable element."

It was my senior-year philosophy teacher who told me to read Primo Levi's *If This Is a Man*. We discussed it afterward, and what he said was essentially: "You know, we're all the more shocked by the antisemitic laws because they were directed at people who thought they were well integrated in European societies. It was our neighbors across the hall being persecuted. But during the 1930s, weren't these same racist laws—although there was no question of extermination—being applied by the English to unskilled laborers in India and by the French to Blacks in Africa, and nobody was shocked by that?"

Everyone needs a philosophy teacher who's read Aimé Césaire. I don't know if he was Jewish. These questions weren't being asked at the time, so they just weren't questions you asked. But I've remembered something else from him, this dark story that is the quintessence of Ashkenazi humor and encapsulates the attitude of Jews confronted with a hostile world.

1942. Two Jews are facing a firing squad.

One of them calls to the Nazi officer and demands a blindfold. His friend looks at him and says, "Stop. You'll only make trouble for us."

In the fall of 1972, when I was reading Primo Levi's book, a party was founded in France, on October 5 to be exact: the Front National. This, of course, was the "new" one, not the real one that had been part of the Resistance, given that the far right always likes scrambling useful markers, dismantling the meaning of words, and tainting them in the process.

Among its members were plenty who'd escaped the sinking Nazi ship and had long since been freed: the man who registered its statutes—along with a more presentable former Poujadistic politician, Jean-Marie Le Pen—was named Pierre Bousquet. Bousquet was one of the thirty Waffen-SS in the Charlemagne Division who protected Hitler's bunker in Berlin from Red Army soldiers right to the very end in April 1945.

The FN's first secretary was named Victor Barthélemy: he was second-in-command in Doriot's French Popular Party, the PPF, and a founding member of the Legion of French Volunteers Against Bolshevism, the notorious LVF, who'd worn German uniforms and had joined forces with the Waffen-SS Charlemagne. Barthélemy, a militiaman and zealous backup to the police during the roundup of Jews at the Vel' d'Hiv, a Paris Velodrome, took refuge in Mussolini's short-lived and blood-soaked Republic of Salo in 1944, and in early 1945 he tried to found a "white maquis" in France. Once imprisoned, despite being a civilian, he managed to be tried by a military court: a good choice—he served only a few months in prison.

We mustn't forget André Dufraisse, the FN's cofounder who'd also been a member of the LVF and had then served in a German armored division on the Eastern Front. This earned him the nickname "Uncle Panzer" with his friends in the Front National.

It would be easy to make a lengthy list of these French former Nazis who were present for the founding of this ancestor to the National Rally: Léon Gaultier, cofounder of the FN, had, some years earlier, been the "holy of holies of the Waffen-SS," to use the words of Jean Mabire in his hagiography of this army corps; Roland Gaucher, a member of the FN's steering committee who, writing under his real name of Roland Goguillot in *Le National populaire* in 1944, said that "antisemitic legislation is guilty of substantial omissions. It does not go far enough, it is not assiduous"; François Brigneau, the FN's first vice president, a racist and antisemitic propagandist in *La Fronde* whose "manifesto" refused to allow "nomads who have been more or less Gallicized by the *Journal officiel* to call the shots in our country"; and Pierre Gérard, the FN's secretary-general in 1980 who, under the Vichy government, had been second-in-command in the senior management of "economic Aryanization" and director of propaganda for the General Commission on the Jewish Question.

I've missed some, but I'm done with them.

That's a definite no; clemency isn't my forte. On monuments to the dead, it says that André, Célestin, and so many others "died for France"; in that case, these people lived against her, and so do those who have succeeded them and who perpetuate their obsessions.

There is no debating such ideas, there can be no polite war of words, but rather a true war waged against them. Because democracy is a conversation between civilized people; tolerance comes to an end with intolerance. Whoever sows hatred for another doesn't deserve the hospitality of discussion. Whoever wants inequality in the human race has no right to equality in the discussion. This pithy formula from the historian and Resistance fighter Jean-Pierre Vernant works for me: "You don't talk recipes with cannibals."

De Natura Humanitatis

HOW COULD THE GERMANS claim to know nothing about the horrors of the camps and the extermination of the Jews?

And if they knew, how could they accept it all?

These two simple questions, which also apply to the French, were asked by a student at Cubberley High School in Palo Alto, California, in April 1967 during a conversation with his history teacher after a lesson about the Third Reich. The teacher then had a strange idea: to re-create Nazi Germany in miniature in his classroom in the space of just a week.

There's a chance you've already heard about this social experiment, because it spawned a movie in 1981, *The Wave*; another one in Germany in 2008, *Die Welle*; two documentaries, *Lesson Plan* and *The Invisible Line*; and even a Netflix series, *We Are the Wave*. If all that has passed you by, I owe it to myself to tell you about it, along with a few other experiments. If not, then, as with Choose Your Own Adventure books, you can skip a few paragraphs.

First, I need to introduce the teacher, Ron Jones: he was a one-off. The previous year, to teach his students about "trust," he'd divided them into pairs with one student leading around the other, who was blindfolded; and to get them to experience racial segregation in their everyday lives, he'd forbidden randomly selected students from using some of the high school's restrooms.

On the Monday morning in question, Jones started his lesson by ordering the whole class to sit "properly," then to practice being as quick as possible when standing up, sitting down, and zigzagging between the desks. He told them to read a passage and then asked them to talk about it while respecting strict rules: they must stand at attention, start by saying "Mr. Jones," and express themselves concisely. If anyone stammered, they had to start over until they could be clear and concise. Jones was afraid the students would revolt. But they didn't. Quite the opposite, in fact: the class participated eagerly. Even the usual rebels became model students. And they all listened attentively to one another.

When Jones came into the classroom that Tuesday, all the students were already there, sitting at their desks, focused, not one of them smiling. Jones wrote "Strength through Discipline" on the chalkboard, and then, underneath it, "Strength through Community," then he spoke at length. They hung on his every word. He suggested a name, the "Third Wave," because he said that in a succession of waves, "the third was always the most powerful." The name was snappy, and no one spotted the similarity to the Third Reich ... Jones suggested a "salute," a hand curled over its palm, like a wave about to break. The students were to salute him like this and show pride in being part of the group.

One girl in the class resisted. This first "breaker" was excluded and sent to the library "for a semester." The students were not allowed to discuss her exclusion or to talk to her outside the classroom. Jones had just invented his "opponent." Angry and humiliated, the excluded student went home, made posters against the Third Wave, and hung them on the school walls during the night.

First thing on Wednesday morning, the students tore down all her posters, unprompted. Ron Jones wrote "Strength through Action" on the chalkboard and handed out membership cards with a wave logo. Members of the Third Wave had to take up positions in the school corridors to "recruit" more adherents. A girl from a different class jeered at one of them, and when the recruiter asked repeatedly for her name, she refused to give it. They came close to exchanging blows... Jones also handed out three special cards stamped with a red X: students with these cards were to report anyone who didn't respect "the Wave's rules." There were only three cards, but twenty students informed on friends and relations. The "trials" started that afternoon, with the accused stepping up onto the school stage: "You've been seen talking to revolutionaries," Jones announced. The accused filed onto the stage one after another. "Guilty!" screamed the whole class, and the rebels were excluded. They joined the other breaker in the library for the semester.

———

Meanwhile, Jones was becoming increasingly anxious. In just three days the atmosphere in the school had become electric, and violence was about to erupt...Along came Thursday.

So many students were skipping class so they could attend Jones's lessons that his class had swelled from thirty to eighty students. Jones told them, "The Third Wave is part of a national youth movement, a new party is about to be established." The teenagers listened enthusiastically. "At midday tomorrow, Friday," Jones continued, "one of the leaders will announce its official inception. The school will be holding a rally in the auditorium." A peculiar coincidence lent his words some credibility: a full-page ad in that week's *Time* magazine referred to a product—a cleaning product!—called "Third Wave" with the slogan "The Third Wave is coming."

Come midday on Friday, the "movement" could boast two hundred members sitting bolt upright on benches in the auditorium, whose walls were covered in Third Wave banners. Jones gave a brisk salute, and two hundred arms gave the "wave" salute. Then Ron Jones turned on the television set and snow fuzzed across the screen for a long time. Disciplined and obedient, the students waited. Several minutes crawled past. Eventually, someone asked a question: "There's no leader at all, is there?" Jones shook his head and started to talk. Having been harsh, his voice became gentle: "You're right. But I'm sure we would all have made good Nazi Germans."

He then showed them a film about the Third Reich: the pomp and protocol of the NSDAP's conventions, the *Volk*, race, discipline, obedience. Next came images of violence, terror, and gas chambers. The students were mortified. "Just like the Germans," Jones said, "you find it hard to admit you went so far. You don't want to admit you were manipulated. You wouldn't admit you were part of such madness."

I've spoken to a former student from that tenth-grade class at Cubberley High School. His name is Mark Hancock, and the Third Wave made a lifelong impression on him. Mark is no longer fifteen years old and Ron Jones is no longer his teacher, but they've stayed friends. Mark and a few others created a website, The Wave Home, subtitled "Be careful who you follow because you never know where they will lead you" in the hope that what they had learned to their own detriment could be useful for others.

But what had they learned? That if democracy is so fragile, then the individual is vulnerable when confronted with the masses. That our aptitude to form groups may have saved humanity when we lived in tribes, but it also created the conditions for our own subservience. Jones's students were so quick to abandon their freedom, so eager to be a part of something greater than themselves. For some of them, the Third Wave was their salvation, their life even. At last they had some power. Over other people, but over themselves too. And yet, because they'd been tricked, they now felt like victims of this Third Wave in which they themselves had been actors.

Mark Hancock owns a German soldier's World War II helmet. A relic handed down to him by his father. He looks at it sometimes and always wonders what went on inside the mind of that soldier who must have so loved the "carnivals of metal with torches and pennants hung with bells," described by the humorist Pierre Desproges.

My teenage years weren't devoid of flags. Mine were red, stamped with the hammer and sickle whose design was inspired by Vera Mukhina's statue *Worker and Kolkhoz Woman*, a slender, almost abstract sickle so different from the ones wielded by communists and "Mao-Stals." But seeing those flags in their hundreds fluttering amid the raucous ardor of rallies was always a source of an obscure discomfort that I couldn't decipher. Victory needed large numbers, but seeing individuals dissolving into a crowd was a form of defeat. This conflict between the necessary and the irreconcilable always stifled my enthusiasm and kept me at arm's length.

Before and after the Third Wave experiment, there were many others. They all show what peculiar social animals we are, how malleable and vulnerable; manipulating us is child's play. Absolutely anyone becomes incompetent if subjected to repeated failure. And someone who is spontaneously altruistic in their connection with another person becomes indifferent if that other person is made inferior. And, relieved of responsibility for the crime, the altruist can turn torturer.

Stanley Milgram's experiment, which was also carried out in the 1960s, is famous. There's even a now forty-year-old Henri Verneuil film, *I as in Icarus*, that depicts it.

It features three protagonists: First, a "student," who is in fact an actor and is tasked to memorize a certain number of words; second, a "teacher," the true subject of the experiment, who dictates the words, checks the answers, and, when there's a mistake, administers an electric shock to the student. This punishment can go right up to four hundred fifty volts, causing loss of consciousness or worse. The shocks are imaginary, the actor-student pretends to be in pain, but the teacher doesn't know this. Last, and this is crucial, a scientist who is also an actor and whose white lab coat confirms his status: he is the "supervisor," he represents authority, and his role is to push the teacher if and when he or she hesitates. Three out of four teachers went all the way up to administering four hundred fifty volts to the student.

Milgram's experiment has been repeated many times and has always produced similar results. Everyone, or nearly, can become a torturer if there's a higher authority to relieve them of all responsibility. An innocent torturer. *Nicht schuldig.* I don't know at what point the "good student" that I was would have stopped, but I like to think I would have been able to resist the supervisor's pressure. And I think André would have been more humane than I would.

One last extraordinary experiment and then I'll be done with them, promise. It was broadcast by the National Geographic channel as part of its show *Brain Games*. The producers published a small ad offering a free eye checkup. A young woman replied to the ad and would become the test subject.

When she arrived in the waiting room for her appointment, half a dozen patients were already sitting there, waiting.

She sat down on an empty chair. There was a sudden short beeping sound, and, to her surprise, everyone stood up and sat straight back down. Of course, the other patients were actors, and the experiment had begun. A few minutes later there was another beep: they stood up and sat down. Time went by, another beep. This time the young woman stood up along with them. She was conforming to the herd's rules. The process continued with a succession of beeps and stand-sits; her social apprenticeship was underway, but now the actors started leaving the room one by one, summoned by the nonexistent ophthalmologist. Eventually, she was alone. There was a beep, and she still stood up. A newcomer arrived, another beep, she stood up, sat back down, and—because he expressed his surprise—she "taught" him the required behavior, although of course she couldn't explain its logic. As the experiment went on, more "patients" arrived, summoned by the production team, and there wasn't a single actor left. Now a whole roomful of people obeyed the beep's implied instruction.

We are conformist and mimetic primates. Our brains instinctively know there's power in numbers, and under invisible pressure from our "peers"—even though they may be complete strangers—we adopt their behaviors. It's a source of comfort: resistance would require effort, the beginnings of rebellion.

I don't know whether we're spontaneously "fascist," whether it's in our nature to abdicate in the face of force, authority, and collective pressure. In his novel *Man's Hope*, André Malraux shows the communist character Manuel talking to Alba, a former fascist who's joined the Spanish Republicans; but Manuel still doesn't trust her, and Malraux has him say that "deep down, fascists always believe in the race of whoever's in command." Manuel adds that "a man who's both active and pessimistic is where you would expect to see a fascist, except there's some loyalty in the background."

Perhaps we need to choose our loyalties and stick to them. Perhaps never succumbing to the notion of other people's inferiority is supreme loyalty to what makes us human. To maintain our humanity, we should probably always smile when a beggar appeals directly to us. I don't always do that.

Of course, when we're confronted with the otherness that typifies other people, we're "naturally" afraid. There would be no hens left if chicks weren't wary of the cat. But the ancient Greeks, who—to our modern sensibilities—weren't paragons of virtue, still said that when someone comes knocking at your door, it could be a god coming to ask if you're free to go with them.

Eden and Paradise

I HAD AN URGE to picture André and Simone as two happy ghosts in a bygone Dieulefit, a place not so different from the village today; an urge to see them laugh, dance, sing... and I researched what they might have watched at the movies, listened to on the radio or on phonographs, what would have been the soundtrack to their lives at a time when there were a lot of sounds, but not yet a "track." Because we're not twenty for long, and it's our duty to refuse to be robbed of our youth by war and dictatorship.

It was only natural that life should go on even if, as Walter Benjamin said, "That things are 'status quo' is the catastrophe." On the stage at the Moulin Rouge in Paris, Mistinguett was singing "La Tour Eiffel est toujours là" (the Eiffel Tower's still there), because, as the song goes:

Paris, my Paris, how different your face is
Your streets are quiet and your taxis

Stand idle around
On the avenue du Bois
Women with their shoes made 'f wood
Walking on the paving slabs 'f wood
Make a tap-dancing sound
But there's the same brightness in your sky
Your heart hasn't changed to my eye
To see that, I've found,
We need only look around.

The singers of the day were Édith Piaf, Jean Sablon, Tino Rossi, Georges Guétary…At the Folies Bergère, Charles Trenet—who "made songs like an apple tree makes apples"—was singing "Douce France" (sweet France). Some saw it as a song of resistance because the audience joined in; others as Pétainist, also because the audience joined in. That question can never be resolved, but no one ever found traces of a Resistance network at the Folies Bergère.

The Germans certainly didn't envisage closing Paris restaurants, music halls, or brothels. Occupied Paris was to remain a city of pleasure, a place for the troops to relax; after all, the capital was there for the taking, consenting to defeat and surrendering eagerly to its new masters.

The curfew enforced in the occupied zone from February 1942 left us the forgotten expression of being "called Arthur" for being reprimanded, because German soldiers admonished stragglers with cries of "*Acht Uhr!*"—the German for "eight o'clock" sounds similar to the French pronunciation of "Arthur." But in actual fact, the curfew was much later in cities; in Paris it was midnight, and, so long as you caught "the last métro," as per François Truffaut's movie, you could be home just before breaching it. The Lido, the Casino de Paris, and the Moulin Rouge turned people away every evening. At Maxim's, the Tour d'Argent, and La Marée, the victors paid half price, and they dined in these restaurants with collaborators and black marketeers, as well as anyone—and there were plenty—who could afford a meal that cost several days' pay. "Heute! Ganz Gross! Hinein!" runs the ad outside the A.B.C. Theater on boulevard Poissonnière.

The Germans were there, and, to state the obvious, the performers who weren't somewhere else were there too. When Arletty said how shocked she was to see a huge swastika on the Champs-Élysées, Sacha Guitry replied: "Well, we can't get them out, so let's try to keep them in."

All these decades after the Occupation, it would be inappropriate for anyone who can't act or sing themselves to claim that an actor or singer should have refused to tread the boards... It's possible to write under a pseudonym, but you try playing Feydeau on the quiet. Had I lived in those times and written novels, I would most likely have tried to get them published, weary of waiting for a hypothetical liberation of France. Would my spinelessness and compromising behavior have stopped at that? Would I have gone so far as to have work published by Éditions Balzac—as Jean Anouilh did with his *Pièces noires* and Robert Brasillach with *Les Quatre jeudis*—knowing that this "Balzac" company, which had previously been called Calmann-Lévy, had been "Aryanized," in other words stolen from Jews and entrusted to gangsters? In his *Aurais-je été résistant ou bourreau?* (Would I have been a Resistance fighter or a persecutor?), Pierre Bayard answers this and other questions extremely well, because he leaves the reader to reply to them.

So, short of handing out "Resistance diplomas," let's say it was ill-advised of André Dassary to sing "Maréchal, nous voilà!" (here we are, Marshal), however accurate it may have been. With hindsight, it was insensitive. Just shy of this line in the Nazi sand, which plenty of people stepped over, there's an "artistic" blur, a murky gray area—a Feldgrau area, even—which, if you have any idols, is best left undisturbed.

I knew that Édith Piaf, who was already very famous, continued to perform at the A.B.C. How to resign yourself to the shadows when you're in the limelight? To resist the boards when you're from the streets? In the audience, Nazi uniforms mingled with tailcoats from wealthy neighborhoods, and they all listened to her sing "Where are they now, my friends who went off to war one morning?" and give her rendition of "Un Coin tout bleu" (a hint of blue) and "Tu es partout" (you are everywhere). Piaf also toured in Germany, and was criticized for it. What I didn't know was that she'd chosen to live on the fourth floor of a luxury brothel, an extremely chic bordello where the residents and visitors—German officers, collaborators, and members of the Gestapo, whose headquarters were moments away on the rue Lauriston—uncorked champagne bottles with sabers and slathered their caviar on thickly. Olivier Dahan's biopic *La Vie en rose*, starring Marion Cotillard, nimbly skips over these less than glorious five years. I'd always associated Paul Meurisse, whom I admire, with the Resistance, perhaps because several years later he portrayed Resistance leaders in Julien Duvivier's *Marie-Octobre* and then Melville's *Army of Shadows*. He was a good actor, and life, like black-and-white films, is actually a shifting palette of grays.

It's a long way from the Parisian boulevard Poissonnière to rue du Bourg in Dieulefit. But songs travel, and perhaps Simone sang along to Irène de Trebert's "Mademoiselle Swing," and André to Reda Caire's "Swing, Swing, Madame," two hits from before 1943, the year the Vichy government decided to ban swing... "I remember Reda Caire," Georges Perec begins in his book *I Remember*.

Surely, Simone and André even had a friend with more

money to spare, the lucky owner of a portable phonograph, perhaps a hand-cranked His Master's Voice gramophone player. And they would take it with them into the *bories* to dance the night away to a handful of 78s of "degenerate" American jazz. Maybe they kissed to some Glenn Miller, "Moonlight Serenade," or as they listened to "Summertime" sung by Billie Holiday? I'd like to think so.

On the other hand, there's little chance that, as the two sweethearts strolled around Dieulefit, they would ever meet one of the long-haired *zazous* who sauntered down the Boul'Mich (boulevard Saint Michel) in Paris or took a table on the Pam-Pam terrace on the Champs-Élysées. In *Vercoquin et le plankton*, Boris Vian describes the specimen in question like this: "The male sported a curled mop of hair and a sky-blue suit with a jacket down to the calves...The female also wore a jacket and peeping at least a millimeter below it a full pleated skirt in Mauritian tarlatan." The *zazou* was a strange species, probably an expression of rebellion from the dandyish gilded youth of Paris who rejected Vichyite conformity without wanting to truly commit to anything.

No, I can't see André and Simone as *zazous*. And myself, as a young Parisian, in this outfit? I hope not. Luckily, the prerequisite mane of curly hair would have been a stumbling block.

✝

Dieulefit had a movie theater, the Eden. There still is one, the Labor, but the Eden has gone. It was replaced by the hospital, and its programming from the time of the Occupation was lost when the building was destroyed. It would be pointless hoping to find ads in the local papers. Why waste paper advertising the movies they were showing when it was impossible for people to get there with no gas and no cars? At the time, there was just one car for every twenty inhabitants in France, and one for every forty in the Drôme region. There were fewer than ten in La Paillette, and most of those were utility vehicles belonging to tradesmen. Perhaps Jean Chaix, being a baker, had an old Peugeot 201 T. But why burn fuel to go to the movies, when there were bicycles?

Luckily, the Comité d'Organisation de l'Industrie Cinématographique (one of a number of organizations set up by the Vichy regime to run the French economy, in this instance the movie industry) has kept a partial record of what was screened: more than sixty films in less than four years. Judging from the list, even in its incomplete state, the programming was one or even two years behind Paris. *The End of the Day*, Julien Duvivier's wonderfully cruel 1939 comedy with Louis Jouvet and Michel Simon, wouldn't be screened until March 1942. Henri Decoin's *The Strangers in the House*, with Raimu, Juliette Faber, and the admirable Noël Roquevert, was shown in late October 1942. But there's every reason to think that the Eden changed its program almost weekly and promised at least three or four screenings each time.

This is because during the Occupation, France—which was short of potatoes, gasoline, coal, and valor—still went to the movies. In spite of everything, the number of visits to movie theaters remained almost the same as before the war, when every month every French citizen went, on average, almost four times more frequently than they do today.

Of course, some actors and directors had emigrated— from Jean Renoir to René Clair and Louis Jouvet to Michèle Morgan—but many had stayed, and all of them, or almost, continued to work: the directors Marcel L'Herbier, Henri-Georges Clouzot, and Claude Autant-Lara, and the actors Fernandel, Raimu, Fernand Gravey, Arletty, Jules Berry, Pierre Brasseur...To be absolutely honest, national film production was having a golden age: competition from Britain and the United States had evaporated, and, because moviegoers stayed away from the big German propaganda machines, four in every five films was French. Nearly two hundred movies were shot in four years.

For Christmas 1941 the Eden screened two American films from the late thirties and early forties, *Zorro Rides Again* and *The Mark of Zorro*. A minor digression for the sake of cinephiles: the future Indiana Jones would borrow a good deal from the hero of these two movies featuring Zorro, who wasn't in fact Zorro, alias Diego de la Vega, but his nephew: James Vega, airplane pilot, skyscraper climber, and importantly, like Harrison Ford, very adept with a whip. That holiday week also saw screenings of the now long-forgotten *Coral Reefs* with Jean Gabin and Michèle Morgan.

Censorship was scarcely a concern for the Eden's pro-grammer: as of December 7, when the United States entered the war after the Japanese attack on Pearl Harbor, American films were banned. And six months earlier Morgan had left France for Hollywood, soon to be joined by Gabin; the review *Photoplay* even published a piece about him under the title "Escaped from the Nazis." A strange end to the year for a country under the Vichy thumb, but the authorities probably had bigger fish to fry than monitoring the Eden's programming.

In the list of films, many of which mean nothing to me—*Son oncle de Normandie*, anyone? Or *Berlingot en compagnie?*—one catches the eye: Jean Delannoy's *Gambling Hell*. It was shot in 1939, the German invasion interrupted its release, and it had to wait until 1942 before it was screened. But this film that Simone and André (perhaps) saw—that's right, I've decided that, occasionally, when he was on leave, André went to the movies—was a version that had been cut and put back together by German censorship. Now we're plumbing the depths of Nazi obsessiveness: they insisted the director reshoot every scene featuring the famous actor who chose to call himself "the man you love to hate"—Erich von Stroheim, the terrific German officer in Jean Renoir's *The Grand Illusion*. Yes, reshoot them because, despite the aristocratic "von" that he'd added to his name, Stroheim was Jewish. Jean Delannoy agreed to erase him.

Von Stroheim couldn't have cared less; he was in the United States, performing in *Arsenic and Old Lace* on Broadway. But the irony is that he would still have his revenge: in 1943, American movie theaters would screen *Five Graves to Cairo*, a Billy Wilder film in which he played Field Marshal Erwin Rommel himself, another "man you love to hate."

Von Stroheim and Billy Wilder, also a German émigré, are both incarnations of Wilder's terrible reply when he was asked whether he was an optimist or a pessimist: "A pessimist. The pessimists are in Hollywood. The optimists are in Auschwitz."

Even though I can't see it on the list, it's likely that in early 1944, the Dieulefitois were able to watch *The Fantastic Night*, Marcel L'Herbier's great success of 1942. I like to think that as they emerged from the darkened theater, Simone might have laughed as she told André: "Oh, how you talk, you're like a dictionary…" Did the two youngsters enjoy *The Murderer Lives at Number 21*, Henri-Georges Clouzot's wonderful movie released in 1942? And Maurice Tourneur's *The Devil's Hand* and Abel Gance's *Captain Fracasse*? Did they have a chance to see *The Devil's Envoys*? Did they discuss Marcel Carné's decision to set the action in the Middle Ages to circumvent German censorship? Would they have accepted today's reading of it in which the vulgate claims that Baron Hugues represents Pétain, the devil Hitler, and the lovers Resistance fighters whose hearts still beat under the stone when they are turned to statues in the very last scene?

Perhaps. But Simone and André couldn't watch the costliest film of the war years, *Titanic*, financed by Goebbels. Because yes, before Leonardo DiCaprio and Kate Winslet, there were Sybille Schmitz and Hans Nielsen. And before James Cameron there was Herbert Selpin. This is yet another aside, but you're used to them by now.

Joseph Goebbels wanted a splendid anti-British propaganda film, a big-budget movie to illustrate the cupidity of Anglo-Saxon stockholders and to glorify the German nation. To recap the screenplay: flouting all security measures and despite warnings from the courageous German officer Petersen, the odious owner Bruce Ismay rushes to launch his luxury liner into the Atlantic Ocean. Standing in its path is an iceberg—and no, that's not a Jewish name, as claimed by a famous joke that is about as predictable as the iceberg itself. What happens next is familiar, cold, and salty. Despite widespread panic, Petersen saves as many passengers as he can, even, magnanimously, the loathsome Ismay so that he can be accountable for his crimes.

Goebbels arranged for a refurbishment of the *Cap Arcona*, a magnificent decommissioned liner that was rusting in the Baltic naval base of Gotenhafen. And the head of propaganda chose Herbert Selpin as director. Selpin had been an assistant on Murnau's *Faust* in the 1920s before working for the Fox Film Corporation. Hitler's dictatorship and the exile of the greats—from Fritz Lang to Billy Wilder, Marlene Dietrich, and Peter Lorre—gave opportunities to plenty of second fiddles. What's more, Selpin had already made some propaganda films; he'd even, and this was the clincher, directed maritime scenes.

Goebbels expected a great deal from the filming of *Titanic* and did everything to ensure it succeeded. Hermann Goering even criticized him for stripping out the Eastern Front by recruiting so many men as extras. It was a miscalculation: the Kriegsmarine's sailors were mostly drunken brutes, and there were rapes in the wings, thefts of equipment, brawls, and drunkenness on set. The filming, which started in early 1942 and was scheduled to take a month, initially dropped slightly behind schedule, then dramatically so. Selpin was exasperated, and over dinner one summer's evening with his friend and co-screenwriter for the film Walter Zerlett-Olfenius, he was a little tipsy and started rambling about discipline in the German Army, the future of the Third Reich, and Joseph Goebbels's intelligence—ill-fated recklessness, because Zerlett-Olfenius reported him to the Gestapo. Selpin had to explain himself to Goebbels. He was accused of defeatist remarks and arrested on July 31, 1942.

He was sent to the Alexanderplatz police headquarters in Berlin for the night and in the morning was found dead in his cell, hanged by his suspenders. On Goebbels's orders, the Gestapo had instructed two of its men to assassinate him.

A director with a still lower profile, Werner Klingler, formerly of Universal Studios, took over filming the last scenes and the editing. But it was already February 1943. Germany, which had so far been spared from the war it was waging with the entire world, was now being bombed by the Allies from Hamburg to Berlin. The scenes of panic depicted in the disaster movie were reminders of similar scenes in German cities. At the first private screening, Goebbels thought the film too defeatist and decreed that it wouldn't be released on the Reich's territory. Parisians, on the other hand, would see it in late 1943, but without the name Selpin in the credits.

Titanic was intended to be a metaphor for the collapse of Great Britain. Its filming turned into a catastrophic and pitiful allegory for Nazi Germany.

André and Simone would never have seen *Titanic*, but I so wish they could have discovered *Children of Paradise*, and Simone could have mimicked Arletty, whispering in her lover's ear, "Dieulefit is so small for people like us who love each other with such great love." Marcel Carné had finished filming the movie at the Victorine Studios in Nice on June 20, 1944, two days after Simone's father, Célestin Reynier, died. The director had overcome all manner of obstacles: Vichy had banned movies of more than 2,700 meters of film, but *Children of Paradise* would have 5,000 meters and a three-hour run time. With satin and velvet nowhere to be found, the costumiers used furnishing draperies, which weren't rationed. Lastly, the excessive cast suffered some defections, including the actor Robert Le Vigan, a notorious antisemite who, sensing that the winds were changing, fled to Sigmaringen with Louis-Ferdinand Céline and a few others.

France was liberated, and *Children of Paradise* wouldn't be released until 1945. And the film, like Goebbels's *Titanic*, was a parable, a reflection of the mosaiclike complexities of France at the time: Jacques Prévert, a fellow traveler to the French Communist Party, worked for the Resistance; the homosexual Marcel Carné used a dummy company to employ two remarkable Hungarian Jews, the composer Joseph Kosma and the set designer Alexandre "Trau" Trauner, both of whom had already worked with the Carné-Prévert duo on *The Devil's Envoys*; Jules Berry would squander his money at the casino in Nice; and Arletty, who was pregnant by a German officer, had an abortion during the filming. She would be pardoned after the war because everybody knew "her heart [was] French and her ass international."

Even though they were released two years apart, it feels appropriate to have mentioned the filming of these two movies—*Titanic* and *Les Enfants du paradis*—in parallel: the first shot in an atmosphere of terror, the other in one of freedom "in spite of…"

Because, during the Occupation, nothing was created without an "in spite of," sometimes an "against," and everything was a case of "making do."

André, Jules and Jim

WHEN I DISCOVERED from André's cousin Huguette that he smoked a pipe, and did so "very elegantly," Henri Roché's face came to me. In his portrait by Man Ray, he too is smoking a pipe "very elegantly." Chancing across Roché on the rue du Bourg, André would inevitably have been impressed by the sheer presence of this already aging man.

Henri Roché, also known as Henri-Pierre Roché, proceeded through the century so discreetly that it's perfectly fair not to know his name. Firstly, let's say that in 1953 he published his first book, *Jules et Jim*—very late in the day, because he was seventy-four. François Truffaut's film, released nearly ten years later, is far more famous than Roché's modestly successful book, and the author died in 1959 without seeing it. But Truffaut had had time to show him a photograph of the proposed actress, and Roché had deemed that, yes, Jeanne Moreau would make a wonderful Kathe.

But where was the first paragraph of *Jules et Jim* written? In Dieulefit, twelve years earlier, in 1941.

Henri Roché, then. He was first and foremost an incredible networker, and very many people met thanks to him. A dandy of independent means at the turn of the twentieth century, Henri was twenty when he became a regular at the Bateau-Lavoir in Montmartre and La Ruche in Montparnasse. He wanted to write but didn't believe in his own talent. Given who he met and befriended, it can't have been easy venturing to be a creative. There's now going to be a lot of name-dropping, so apologies in advance, particularly as some of the names I drop are so famous that first names are superfluous. Henri Roché was friends with Pablo Picasso, Guillaume Apollinaire, Max Jacob, the painter Diego Rivera, Erik Satie, Blaise Cendrars, him again . . . he boxed with the painter André Derain; introduced Gertrude Stein to modern art, telling her to buy Picassos; and lent Man Ray the funds to set up house in Paris. Between the wars, forced to work and to transition from art collector to art dealer, he also befriended Marcel Duchamp and Gaston Gallimard, his future publisher, who said of him that he should have had a great career "but he probably didn't feel that strongly about it."

Most importantly, just before World War I, while at the Closerie des Lilas, he met a talented young idler who was to become his greatest friend: the German writer Franz Hessel, future translator of Proust and father of Stéphane Hessel. Their love story with the same woman, Helen Grund, whom Hessel went on to marry, would provide the framework for

Jules et Jim. Franz would be Jules, Henri Jim, and Kathe was an incarnation of Helen, who, in the real world, did not take her own life. All of Roché's books from *Jules et Jim* to *Deux anglaises et le continent*—another Truffaut film—revolve around the sun of free love, friendship, and complicated feelings.

Roché most likely started writing *Jules et Jim* in Dieulefit in March 1941, because it was there that he'd learned of Franz's death two months earlier. Hessel had just been released from the Camp des Milles internment camp for "enemies" of the Reich, an antechamber to Auschwitz near Aix-en-Provence. Free, yes. But he didn't survive the dysentery he'd contracted there.

Henri-Pierre Roché stayed in Dieulefit for three years. So yes, André and Simone would often have come across this "Monsieur Roché," a distinctive figure in a small-town environment, an elegant sixtysomething with a tall, almost thin frame and an aquiline profile. Roché taught at the school in Beauvallon and was even given accommodation there with his wife, Denise, and son, Jean-Claude. In exchange for an hour of English conversation with the teenage students every Monday, he was provided with a bedroom-cum-study in the attic, where he wrote his novel. But he also taught them chess, the "sport" that he'd played with Marcel Duchamp, as well as gymnastics and, of course, boxing. I was told that André, too, boxed. Could it be that…? It's an unsettling idea, fanciful even, but should we succumb to it?

✝

Much has been written about Dieulefit, the small industrial
and artisanal town that saved so many Jewish children and
teenagers from extermination. Doubtless at Roché's invitation, many artists sought shelter there, and in 1941, nearly
one in three of its inhabitants was a refugee, almost one
for every household: on those streets and café terraces it
was perfectly possible to meet the poets Pierre Seghers and
Pierre Emmanuel, and the philosopher Emmanuel Mounier,
who founded the review *Esprit*. There's a photo of them
smiling as they pose on the edge of the town. You might
also have come across the pianist Yvonne Lefébure, not to
mention those, and there were so many of them, who spent
only a month or two there, such as Louis Aragon and Elsa
Triolet, who were being hunted by the Gestapo. They all
lived on farms and in attic rooms, alongside Austrian Jews,

German communists, and Spanish republicans. During the war, Dieulefit was both a "nest of communists and Jews," according to the Gestapo, and the "intellectual capital of France," if we're to believe the writer Andrée Viollis or the historian Pierre Vidal-Naquet. They may all be right, and the one explains the other.

On the other side of the Rhône, in the Haute-Loire region, is the renowned Le Chambon-sur-Lignon, another town of three thousand souls—the cliché is fully justified in this instance—and its husband-and-wife team, André and Magda Trocmé, who founded the unique and historic secondary school the École Nouvelle Cévenole. Pastor André Trocmé's informal network took in and hid more than three thousand refugees, one-third of them Jews. Among them were the writer André Chouraqui, the historian Léon Poliakov, and the future mathematical genius Alexander Grothendieck, with whom fate had me cross paths thirty years later, when I too was seventeen. As I write this, I know I'm that little human silhouette that's put in photos next to the pyramids to give an idea of their size, but never mind. In 1942, Albert Camus also came to Chambon for a few months; he wrote *The Misunderstanding* there and worked on *The Plague*, which would be published five years later.

In Dieulefit, as in Chambon, solidarity had evolved around a school, the School of Beauvallon. It's a huge, light-colored building built in the early twentieth century, located on the higher ground to the north of the rue des Reymonds, which leads to La Paillette. It was also on the rue des Reymonds that the Dieulefit ceramic works had one of its sites, where André was taken on as an apprentice. Anyone walking into the center of Dieulefit from the School of Beauvallon would have passed the workshops after fifteen minutes.

The school was run by three women: Simone Monnier, Catherine Krafft, and, crucially, Marguerite Soubeyran. The latter was famous: a letter addressed to "Marguerite, in the Drôme," would arrive safely at her door. "Aunt Marguerite" and Catherine Krafft had founded the school in 1929 to take in "difficult children" and allow them to grow up in the pure air of the Drômois hills. The Swiss biologist and psychologist Jean Piaget had come and guided their first steps as teachers. Marguerite had just adopted her son, Guy, and she and Catherine committed to this pilot school in Beauvallon, this "children's republic," as what would now be called a life's work. It had such a high reputation at the time that in March 1943, French *Marie Claire* magazine devoted several pages to this "school of excellence," forgetting to mention that more than half of the students were in fact hidden children in danger of being deported.

Other books describe the establishment's adventures, the women's courage, and their freedom, including in their relationships. Marguerite—a communist, a Protestant, and a lesbian—was a woman of indomitable energy and of courage all the more extraordinary because it was spontaneous. These pages will mention only that during those dark years, the school housed hundreds of children, many of them Jews; that a twenty-year-old secretary at the town hall, Jeanne Barnier, put together thousands of false documents; that the village helped them in silence; and that all this happened when, in early 1941, the Vichy regime had installed a colonel who was in its pocket at the town hall. This Vichyite mayor, Colonel Pizot, stuck the regime's antisemitic posters in the streets, but he knew a lot. When he gave his secretary a promotion in 1943, was it because he'd opted to turn a blind eye, given that the outcome of the war was, shall we say, unpredictable for overzealous collaborators? We have a right to think that Pierre Pizot was in fact unintentionally caught up in a virtuous circle.

The English historian Thomas Fuller wrote that "many would be cowards if they had courage enough." I've always found these words reassuring. If heroism also comprises an element of conformism, well then, I'm absolved of the potential spinelessness I intuit in myself. But of course, Fuller's aphorism says nothing about truly courageous people.

Cowardliness was probably a more difficult trait to have in Dieulefit than in other places. The town did and still does have two communities living side by side: the Roman Catholics, an accepting community, and the Protestants, who matched them in numbers and were historically wealthier. But these "parpaillots" had seen resistance as a tradition since the days of Louis XIV and the *dragonnades* persecutions implemented by a secretary of state for war named Michel Le Tellier and known as Louvois. Catholics and Protestants alike were all solid French republicans and allowed this "miracle of silence," which meant everything could be carried out in the shadows and in broad daylight.

It really was a miracle: despite rumors that Jews and objectors were being housed there, the German Army never decided to sow terror in Dieulefit; not one panzer division, not one *Feldgendarme* would plunder the town or shoot hostages. There would be the occasional Wehrmacht sidecar cutting across the place Charteauras. But with no denunciations, there were no arrests, and the Gestapo didn't come in force as they did in Izieu on April 6, 1944, to round up children. And when a far-reaching operation was mooted in early August, the Allied landings along the Riviera put a stop to it.

After the war, everyone went back to the hurly-burly of his or her life—"la vie et son tourbillon," as the song goes in *Jules et Jim*. Marguerite Soubeyran, Catherine Krafft, and Jeanne Barnier all carried on, not changing a thing. The School of Beauvallon still exists today, modestly pursuing its educational work.

But there was a young man who worked with "Aunt Marguerite" at Beauvallon with whom André must have been friends, and who deserves a mention: François Soubeyran. His name is the clue—Marguerite was his aunt.

That's right, André Chaix could not have *not* known him. François Soubeyran was the son of a farmer in Montjoux; he was only five years older than André and they had similar trajectories. François also joined the FTP in 1943. If André's life hadn't been brutally cut short on August 23, 1944, he—like François—would most likely have joined his fellow Resistance fighters and followed Lattre's First Army all the way to Paris.

What would André have done once he reached the capital? François, who did, would become an actor and would perform Queneau, Kosma, Prévert, and then Vian. Readers who don't recognize his name may now be able to identify this lanky fellow gesticulating onstage in black tights and a red shirtfront. François Soubeyran became "the tall one" in the vocal quartet Les Frères Jacques. When they sang "La Marie-Joseph," he was the vessel's mast, and he was the one acting as a stepladder in *La Confiture* (the jelly). He was also the one with a subtle Drômois accent. When the group disbanded after a near forty-year career, François, then in his sixties, returned to La Paillette to resume another passion of his, ceramics.

So why not dream, why not wonder whether André would have liked to become a fifth Frères Jacques, with, say, a purple shirtfront? Some would argue that the Beatles and the Rolling Stones did a good job of things as foursomes, and I would retort that there were five Beach Boys. I will concede that I should have chosen a better example. But I maintain that everything's plausible, and that fate is a huge joke, a scam even. Why wouldn't someone like André, who could balance upright on a horse, have become a performer?

André in the Maquis

IT'S JUST A TORN-OUT PAGE, folded into quarters, the paper dried, yellowed, and flimsy. You hardly dare touch it. It's inside the "André" box that was entrusted to me. André had stowed it in his leather billfold, so it went everywhere with him.

It's a double-sided page numbered 17 and 18, from a book, *Le Tour de la France par deux enfants* (A tour of France by two children). This novel tells the story of two brothers, André and Julien Volden. André is fourteen, Julien only just seven. They lost their mother a few years earlier, and when their carpenter father also dies, the two orphans have to travel across France to reach an uncle in Marseille. They set out from Phalsbourg, a town in the Lorraine region that was annexed by the Prussians, and there begins a narrative that is both patriotic and republican. In fact, its subtitle is *Duty and Motherland*.

piter : c'est le moyen de retrouver bientôt le vrai sentier.

Quand la brune fut venue, André et Julien se remirent en route, après avoir remercié de tout leur cœur le garde Fritz, qui de son lit leur répétait en guise d'adieu :

« Courage, courage ! avec du courage et du sang-froid on vient à bout de tout. »

VIII. — Le sentier à travers la forêt. — Les enseignements du frère aîné. — La grande Ourse et l'étoile polaire.

> Le frère aîné doit instruire le plus jeune par son exemple et, s'il le peut, par ses leçons.

A l'ouest, derrière les Vosges, le soleil venait de se coucher ; la campagne s'obscurcissait. Sur les hautes cimes de la montagne, au loin, brillaient les dernières lueurs du crépuscule, et les noirs sapins, agitant leurs bras au souffle du vent d'automne, s'assombrissaient de plus en plus.

Les deux frères avançaient sur le sentier, se tenant par la main ; bientôt ils entrèrent au milieu des bois qui couvrent tout cette contrée.

Julien marchait la tête penchée, d'un air sérieux sans mot dire. — A quoi songes-tu, mon Julien ? demanda André.

— Je tâche de bien me rappeler tout ce que disait le garde ; fit l'enfant, car j'ai écouté le mieux que j'ai pu.

— Ne t'inquiète pas, Julien ; je sais bien la route et nous ne nous égarerons pas.

— D'ailleurs, reprit l'enfant de sa voix douce et aiguë, si l'on s'égare, on reviendra tranquillement sur ses pas, sans avoir peur, comme le garde a dit de le faire. N'est-ce pas, André ?

— Oui, oui, Julien, mais il nous faut tâcher de ne pas nous égarer.

— Pour cela, tu sais, André, il faut regarder les étoiles à chaque carrefour ; le garde l'a dit, je t'y ferai penser.

— Bravo, Julien, répondit André, je vois que tu n'as rien perdu de la leçon du garde ; si nous sommes deux à nous souvenir, la route se fera plus facilement.

— Oui, dit l'enfant ; mais je ne connais pas les étoiles par leur nom, et je n'ai pas compris ce que c'est que le grand Chariot.

Millions of schoolchildren would be introduced to this "fluent reader's book," because it first appeared on the curriculum in 1877 and remained there for almost a century, and would run to hundreds of editions, to the delight of its publishers, Éditions Belin, and their bankers. The author was a woman, Augustine Fouillée, but she signed herself *G. Bruno* in a transparent homage to Giordano Bruno, the Copernican philosopher whom the Vatican burned alive for heresy. After 1906, the Dreyfus-supporting Augustine Fouillée removed any references to religion or God from all new editions.

In 121 very short chapters, the book shows how composite the French nation is and what a wealth of history it has. The narrative teaches the reader about difference, which was not yet called otherness or diversity. But its primary aim is to be educational: thanks to "more than 200 instructive engravings for object lessons," the book allowed André Chaix, who of course shares a name with the older of the two brothers, to learn about the life of Vercingétorix as well as how to churn butter, and probably also about movies, which featured in the book shortly after they'd been invented.

And this passage that André must have read over and over again was surely not chosen at random; it describes how knowledge can overcome fear, how maps can save a life:

VIII. — The Path through the Forest. — The Older Brother's Teachings. — The Big Dipper and the Pole Star.

> The older brother has to teach the younger by his example and, if he can, with his lessons.

[...] The two brothers walked along the path, holding hands; they were soon in the heart of the forest that covers the whole region.

Julien was walking with his head tilted down, his expression serious, without a word.

"What are you thinking about, my Julien?" André asked him.

"I'm trying to really remember everything the guard said," replied the child, "because I listened as best as I could."

"Don't worry, Julien. I know the way just fine, and we won't get lost."

"Actually," the child continued in his soft, resigned little voice, "if we do get lost, we can just retrace our steps with nothing to be afraid of, that's what the guard said, wasn't it, André?"

"Yes, yes, Julien, but we'll try not to get lost."

"Well, you know, André, to do that we have to look at the stars at every crossroads. The guard said so, I'll remind you."

"Very good, Julien," replied André. "I can see you didn't miss anything the guard taught us. If we both remember, then it'll be easier to find our way."

"Yes," said the child, "but I don't know the stars by their names, and I didn't understand what he meant by the Big Dipper."

André, his big brother, goes on to explain it to him. Of course, in the book there's an illustration of the constellation, because "it's useful to learn to recognize these stars in the sky, the ones that form the Big Dipper, the Great Bear that the Mesopotamians already described back in their times. Not far from them is the Pole Star, which exactly pinpoints the north and indicates the compass points at night."

The page that André Chaix kept on him is not illustrated. It didn't need to be. The young maquisard recognized the Great Bear, Orion, Cassiopeia, and plenty more. He'd known since childhood that you could get lost on the paths through the Drôme's forests by day or by night. Not that there were so many forests left in 1943: the countryside around villages had been stripped. The ceramic works with its kilns had had its role in this, but heating oil and coal had now been scarce for three years, so people cut down trees to keep warm as they huddled at home under layers of clothes. Since then, holm oaks, beeches, and sweet chestnuts have reclaimed the hillsides.

I would wager that André knew how to whistle as he walked through the woods, and I know what tune he whistled. Maquisards had a rallying song, the theme tune for a *France libre* program, *Honneur et patrie* (Honor and homeland), broadcast by the BBC from May 17, 1943, onward. The tune was whistled on the radio twice a day, specifically so that it could be recognized despite the enemy's scrambling. Not everyone knew by heart the words to "Chant des partisans," written by Joseph Kessel and Maurice Druon, with its "Friend, do you hear the ravens' dark flight over our open plains," but they all knew Anna Marly's stirring melody. It's a good thing that freedom had a tune of its own.

The Morvan maquis also had its own theme, the Camp Marceau hymn, written in November 1943 by the maquisard Georges Navarro.

On the other side of the Alps, a twenty-year-old maquisard, an Italian, was fighting the same war. He'd chosen the pseudonym Santiago because he was born in Santiago de Cuba, and he hadn't yet written *The Baron in the Trees*. Italo Calvino fought alongside his younger brother in the second division of Garibaldi's partisan Brigades. Forced conscription introduced by the Republic of Salò, a puppet regime supported by the Nazis, had thrown them into the war. Until then, the young Italo—perhaps like André—had lived "in a serene, comfortable world," unaware of the ferocity of war. The world seemed to him to be "like an arc comprising different nuances of morality and customs, not opposed to one another, but arranged side by side." War and fascism would steer him to a more radical view.

Calvino has put in an appearance here because I'm thinking of another partisan hymn; it's less saber-rattling than Kessel and Druon's, less strident too, a hymn with words written by the young Italo and music by Sergio Liberovici: "Oltre il ponte." "Over the bridge" describes Italo and André and so many other armed young men brimming with hope:

> We were twenty, and beyond the bridge,
> beyond the bridge that's in the enemy's hands,
> we could see the opposite bank, life,
> all the good in the world beyond the bridge.
> All the evil was facing us,
> all the good was in our hearts.
> At twenty, life is beyond the bridge,
> love begins beyond the fire.

✝

It's a poster that swelled the ranks of maquis units. In the summer of 1942, it was pasted up in every town hall in France and was also very likely to have been in Colonel Pizot's office in Dieulefit: the regular-featured and helmeted face of an Aryan soldier appears against a red twilit sky while two files of workmen seen from behind head toward factories with smoking chimneys. It says:

THEY GIVE THEIR BLOOD
GIVE YOUR WORK
to save Europe from Bolshevism

Germany was short of manpower. Now compelled to reinforce troop numbers on three fronts—North Africa, the Atlantic, and the Urals—Germany forcibly recruited qualified workers in occupied countries. Pierre Laval, then prime minister of France, put the collaboration into operation. In his speech of June 22 in which he famously said, "I hope Germany will be victorious," he instituted the "Change-over," a Vichyite euphemism for requisition. In France, this initially relied on volunteering, but given the lackluster enthusiasm of the French people, Laval introduced a forced conscription law on September 4, 1942. It applied to all men ages eighteen to fifty and all single women ages twenty-one to thirty-five. Laval named this the "Service Obligatoire du Travail" (compulsory work service), or SOT, but because these initials spell the word *sot*—stupid—the scheme was ridiculed, and he renamed it STO a few days later.

But I'm not sure that when André Chaix decided to join the maquis in 1943 it was only due to the STO's threats. In the Drôme, as in plenty of other rural and mountainous départements, the police were a little reluctant to hunt down and forcibly march off the large numbers of young objectors. Everyone knew everyone. The turning point in the war at Stalingrad allowed many to predict Hitler would be defeated and then people would have to account for their actions. In fact, André sometimes spent the night at home, or rather in a cabin at the far end of the bakery's vegetable plot. From there he could have escaped across the fields, should Montélimar's few militiamen have carried out a raid. He never needed to.

And so I would guess that it was more out of personal conviction that he joined the La Lance maquis, named after the mountain that gave it shelter. The farm where he found refuge was at an altitude of nearly one thousand meters, ten kilometers south of La Paillette and as many to the west of Roche-Saint-Secret. The mountain is both huge and wild: it would have been impossible to capture without a whole army, and had there been an attack, the maquisards could have escaped along its valleys as well as over its heights.

Life there was tough: in the barn where the maquisards were hiding, they couldn't light fires, their rations were meager, and their arms limited. All Resistance fighters experienced the triptych of cold, hunger, and fear. Anyone interested can visit the farm today; there's a stone tablet to remember their time there. It's a bucolic setting, making it hard to imagine weapons and gunfire. Trees grow there, oak and box, even a cherry tree. It's been struck by lightning twice, but a branch has always managed to grow back eventually.

André adopted the pseudonym Olivier, a first name but also the name of a tree, an olive tree, that doesn't grow in Germany. He complied with military discipline, an absolute prerequisite for inclusion. The maquis were small units, none comprising more than thirty men, and the one at La Lance was one of the three most active groups. After a few months, André was assigned to the first "Morvan" battalion, named after the man who set them all up. In May 1944, this battalion took in young French objectors to the STO but also a few Spanish republicans and briefly, it seems, an anti-Nazi German. It also included two women, France and Katia, who were explosives experts. As for the head of André's maquis, his name was Monier, and the troop leader was

Marius Audibert, alias Raymond. People here earned their rank according to their organizational skills. And everyone's safety depended on the leaders. It was such an exhausting life that some asked Monier or Morvan to be allowed to return home before they snapped. They were given permission—always—despite the danger of betrayal, of information that might be surrendered under torture.

On the website of the National Resistance Museum, I found a photograph of Raymond posing alongside two maquisards. He's a very young man, and I initially thought it was André. They're in sandals, bare-chested, with what can only be described as mismatched firearms: two hunting rifles and a Mauser C96. The picture was taken in May 1943.

At that time Churchill was still balking at the idea of arming the communists, allies of Stalin's who might choose not to obey Eisenhower. He finally made up his mind when on November 11, 1943, the two hundred maquisards in the Ain region, led by Henri Romans-Petit, achieved a crucial feat: with shouldered arms, they marched to the war memorial monument in Oyonnax and stayed just long enough to lay a sprig of flowers on it. That same day, the Morvan maquis carried out the same operation in Laragne, a small town in the Hautes-Alpes region, and André was most likely one of the forty maquisards who marched there to honor the dead of World War I. By December 1943, London had been persuaded: French Resistance fighters would be armed. The Morvan maquis itself received British rifles, German Mausers, Browning automatic rifles, German MG machine guns, and British light mortars.

Even if only briefly, we should now talk about the maquis' leader, this "Morvan" whom André and two hundred other maquisards obeyed without question. "Yves Morvan" was a pseudonym for Félix Germain, a workman from Marseille, communist, former naval officer, and former member of Spain's International Brigades. Since the beginning of the war, he'd been trying to organize resistance, with no specific instructions from the party. When Hitler invaded the USSR, he threw himself into planning sabotage operations in the Bouches-du-Rhône region. But the Gestapo soon tracked him down; his wife was arrested and deported to Ravensbrück, where, being as strong and brave as Félix, she survived. He had to flee. In early 1943, he took refuge in the Alps, where the leaders of the FTP gave him the rank of captain and entrusted him with the command of Camp Marceau on Faye Mountain. Among the small number of units that he commanded in late 1943 was a Spanish battalion as well as an antifascist Italian one, both of which swiftly crossed the Alps to join Italy's new republican army. All the information I managed to find about Morvan amazed me. He had a gorilla's physique, a Mauser kept in a permanently open case, and five or six grenades dangling around his belt, hung by their pins. Most strikingly, his men, who worshipped him, called him "Chicago" because he drove a Citroën Traction Avant with the wheel rims painted bright red and always had a machine gun between his legs when at the wheel. I like that.

From time to time, the maquisards would settle in a village for a pause, and there they would await instructions from London.

André wrote an undated letter on letterhead paper from the Hôtel-Café Lazare in Sahune, a small town southwest of Montjoux surrounded by mountains.

HOTEL-CAFÉ LAZARE

SAHUNE (DROME)

Sahune, le   194

Bien chers parents deux mots pour vous
dire que vais toujours très bien et j'espère qu'il en est
de même à la maison. Je suis bien content car tous va bien
ici, et l'ont est bien vu par la population civile. J'ai fais
connaissance avec des gens qui connaissent le Paillette
et je suis souvent chez eux si je'y vais pas il vienne me
chercher pour aller veillés chez eux le soir enfin ce sont de
très grand amis pour moi car ce sont des anciens boulanger
qui sont retiré et habite une des plus jolie maison du pays.
Enfin en ce moment pour moi ces des vacances mai je langui
quand même qu'elle ce termine. car tous les 2 jours il
faut prendre 24 heures de garde mais dans le fond ces la pléng
car lorsque on et de garde on ne fait pas de corvé.
Aujourd'hui c'est dimanche et l'ont est au repos. J'espère
avoir une perm, pour dimanche prochain et je conte etre
parmi vous.
        Bien chers parent je termine mon cour bavardage
pour aujourd'hui. Dans l'espoir que ma lettre vous trouvera
tous en bonne santé.
        Recevez de votre fils frère et cousin la plus tendres
affection
        Dédé   Donney pour moi le bonjour au
                                    voisin
                        J'ai écrit a Simone
                        Donney lui bien le bonjour pour
                                    moi

This may seem extraordinarily reckless, but the channels through which it was transmitted were doubtless safe enough. On the envelope are the words "Baker La Paillette":

My dear parents a few words to tell you that I'm still doing very well and I hope the same is true of you at home. I'm really pleased because everything's going well here, and we're well thought of by the civilian population. I've met some people who know La Paillette and I often go to their house if I don't go to them they come and get me to spend the evening with them, anyway they're really good friends to me because they used to be bakers but they're now retired and live in one of the prettiest houses in the area.

Well, it's vacation time for me right now, but I actually can't wait for it to be over because we have to do twenty-four hours on duty every two days but basically we're in hiding because when we're on duty we don't have any fatigues.

It's Sunday today and we're having a day of rest. I'm hoping to get leave for next Sunday and plan to be with you.

My dear parents, I'll end this brief chitchat for today. In the hopes that my letter finds you in good health.

Your son, brother and cousin sends you his warmest affection

Dédé

Say hello to the neighbor from me.
I've written to Simone. Do say hello to her from me.

Here too, I can imagine what it meant to the Chaix parents to have kept a letter like this from their son, such an unremarkable, everyday letter. How often they must have reread it in silence. If the words "civilian population," "duty," and "fatigues" didn't appear in it, no one would suspect it was from a maquisard. It showed me that maquisards could secure leave, could take the time off to spend a Sunday back at home. And go to the movies, then, to see *The Devil's Envoys*. In a photo taken during one such leave, André smiles with his arms around his cousin and his brother. When I found that photo, I knew that this smile would be what I remembered of André.

The routine aspect of the letter is also surprising when you consider the adventure and excitement. But maquisards couldn't be constantly on the offensive, particularly as London wanted them to be available for operations that served her purposes. War, said Jean Gabin, isn't like the movies. One thing they do have in common, though, is that you spend a lot of time waiting.

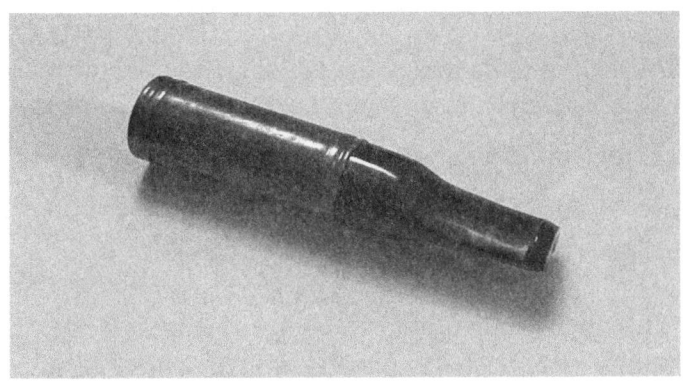

They must have been a little bored, what with the wood chopping and finding provisions. André had time to make himself a cigarette holder out of brass, using a cartridge most likely shot from a Mauser. They must have told one another their own partisan jokes. I can offer you one here. If you've heard it before, then just imagine I'm telling it to André: "Hey, André, have you heard the one about the two Resistance fighters who wanted to assassinate Hitler?"

It's April 1942, and two Resistance fighters have heard that Hitler, who's visiting Budapest, will be crossing a particular bridge. He wants to be driven through the streets standing in the front of his convertible Mercedes before the small waiting crowds. His procession is due to arrive at exactly midday. The two men take up their positions overlooking the bridge well ahead of time, they're crack marksmen, and it will be impossible to miss him from where they are.

At a quarter to twelve, they're completely ready; they wait, fingers on the triggers, eyes glued to their scopes. Five to twelve. Twelve. Twelve-o-five. The procession is a little late.

Twelve ten. Twelve fifteen. No Hitler. Twelve twenty. Still nothing. One of the partisans turns anxiously to his friend and says:

"I hope nothing's happened to him."

✝

The La Lance group is not as well documented as other units in the Morvan maquis, making it difficult to retrace its operations and missions. The Morvan battalions moved around a great deal and were subdivided into small groups, and recollections of who exactly did what have been lost. But we do know that on June 19, three of the maquis battalions—which included André's and comprised just under one hundred men—gave battle to three hundred Germans in a convoy of vehicles in the Hautes-Alpes region's Montclus gorges. There's an "after" photograph that features André. It was a deadly confrontation that lasted two days, and the FTP maquisards had to retreat in the face of greater numbers, but they did succeed in securing some equipment, including two 37-millimeter cannons and their ammunition. These cannons would prove useful against a German detachment in the Saint-Pierre woods on August 22, but that was also the day on which André's 1st Battalion was approaching Grignan and death.

There were lightning-strike operations against militia forces and collaborators, raids that intensified in early 1944 and served as punishment for the massacring of hostages and the murder of Resistance fighters. Expeditious and extrajudicial purges carried out by commandos. Specialist work. André did not take part in these.

Lastly, there were setbacks, the impossible missions. The rescue of deportees on the "ghost train" was one of these failures. "Ghost train" is the nickname given to one of the last deportation convoys to leave France for Dachau. The train was assembled in Raynal, a goods station near Toulouse, on July 1, and nearly five hundred prisoners arrested by the French police were loaded into it. They were mostly Spanish republicans, but also Resistance fighters from the French Secret Army or the MOI, and they included twenty-five women. The heat was stifling. Stuck onto the cattle trucks were signs saying "Horses 8, men 40." Each "40" had been replaced with "70" written in chalk. Watched over by Oberleutnant Baumgartner's SS, this train stood in the station for forty-eight hours before setting off for Bordeaux.

With no food or water, the ordeal was appalling for the prisoners, and the train's peregrinations were insane: from Toulouse to Bordeaux, then Libourne and Angoulême before being forced to return to Bordeaux as the Americans advanced toward the Loire and because of the "green plan" devised by the Guignon maquisards who had destroyed railway lines and liberated the Limousin region. The train trundled slowly back toward Toulouse in order to travel up the Rhône Valley behind the 19th German Army. When the Allies made their first landing on the French Riviera on August 15, six weeks after the train's departure, it was still only at Nîmes.

At every stage, or almost, some died of hunger, some were shot, and more prisoners were forced aboard. Sometimes they were machine-gunned by British Mosquito planes that mistook the train for a military convoy. Prisoners tried waving white rags through gaps in the sides of the cars, to no avail.

On August 18, the train stopped at Châteauneuf-du-Pape in Provence. The bridge had been destroyed, and the prisoners had to walk barefoot along the tracks for five hours under a blistering sun, until they reached Sorgues and picked up another train that took them to Pierrelatte to continue toward Dijon, then Dachau. Unimaginable as it may be, they sang "La Marseillaise" as they walked. Dozens of families in Sorgues who'd heard about the forced march converged on the station with food and water. The Germans were overwhelmed and were wary of opening fire on the crowd; in the confusion a few prisoners managed to escape, wearing railroaders' caps that the staff had lobbed to them. The stationmaster was afraid the Germans would do another count of the prisoners and came up with the idea of sounding the siren. Fearing an aerial attack, the SS reembarked the prisoners without counting them. And the train set off again. The Morvan maquis was not far away; one commando had plans to attack the train, but the 11th Panzer Division's armored vehicles made any sort of intervention impossible. They had to abandon the plan. And, even though the Allies were hot on its heels, the train still reached Dachau.

Among the prisoners on this ghost train were two young brothers, ages twenty and twenty-one, both members of the FTP-MOI, Claude and Raymond Lévy. Thirty years later, Raymond had two children, Marc and Lorraine, who would go on to be a writer and a filmmaker. I was a friend of theirs, and at age eighteen I learned a fragment of this story from their father himself, a man whose life was like a novel. Perhaps this is why, despite the Morvan maquis' failure, I wanted to describe it, however briefly. Raymond and Claude Lévy managed to escape through a hole in the floorboards, dropping down onto the rails one night while the train was in motion. Other, less fortunate escapees were crushed under the wheels of steel. More than two hundred people died on that journey, and of the five hundred prisoners who reached Dachau, half would not return.

No one ever traced SS Oberleutnant Baumgartner.

✝

« MIEUX VAUT MOURIR DEBOUT QUE VIVRE A GENOUX »

INTER E. F.

RÉGION E. 3

FRONT NATIONAL

FORCES FRANÇAISES DE L'INTÉRIEUR

FRANCS TIREURS PARTISANS FRANÇAIS

1ᵉ RÉGIMENT

3ᵉ BATAILLON

Lettre aux Camarades F. T. P. F.

Camarade, dans quelques jours nous allons descendre dans nos grandes villes, les troupes françaises de débarquement ayant entrepris la Libération totale de notre Patrie.

Je sais que la plupart d'entre nous, n'ont que le minimum d'Instruction Militaire, et pourtant nous devons montrer aux Amis Français qui reviennent sur le sol Natal, que nous sommes en temps qu'Armée du Peuple, une Armée organisée et disciplinée. Ce n'est qu'à cette **condition** que l'Armée des Francs-Tireurs et Partisans Français aura la place que son Esprit combatif et ses sacrifices lui donnent droit, dans la future Armée Française.

Quoiqu'étant toujours les premiers au combat nous devons reconnaître que notre discipline, notre correction envers nos supérieurs laissent beaucoup a désirer.

Nous avons déjà, et à plusieurs reprises, expliqué ce que nous, responsables F.T.P.F. entendions par Discipline. Ce que nous voulons obtenir au sein de notre Armée, n'est pas une discipline bôche, c'est une discipline librement consentie comprise et voulue par chacun de nous. Nous devons savoir et comprendre que sans obéissance au Commandement de nos gradés, notre Armée irait irrémédiablement à la défaite et à la désagrégation.

Vous n'ignorez pas Camarade, que pour une Armée la Discipline est la moitié de la Victoire : **et quelle Victoire sera la notre !!!** Une Victoire à laquelle tout homme est fier d'avoir participé : Victoire de la Liberté sur l'Oppression, Victoire des Peuples sur leurs Tyrans terrosses.

De plus, dans les Francs-Tireurs et Partisans Français, nous ne devons pas perdre de vue, que nous ne formons pas uniquement les Forces Française de l'Intérieur. D'autres Officiers commandant l'Armée secrète, collaborent chaque jour avec nos Officiers. Ces Officiers n'ont pas la même conception que nous F.T.P. de l'Armée et de la discipline. Ils risquent d'être facheusement impressionnés par un manque de correction de votre présentation ou de votre salut. Tout cela, Camarades, contribuera à l'opinion QUE SE FERA DE NOUS le Peuple de France, et ses responsables.

Si donc, nous vous demandons de saluer et de prendre une tenue correcte lorsque vous vous adressez à vos Commissaires ou Responsables ce n'est pas un geste d'humiliation ou de soumission que vous aurez à faire ; c'est un geste qui de votre part doit être spontané. Vous connaissez vos Chefs, ils ont vécu comme la plus part d'entre vous de long mois dans le Maquis. S'ils ont aujourd'hui une responsabilité, c'est la Confiance que vous leur portiez qui le leur a donné. Nous les aimions alors. Aujourd'hui respectons-les, sans pour cela amoindrir notre esprit de franche Camaraderie. Saluons nos responsables, ils n'oublient pas ce qu'ils étaient il y a quelques mois encore, et en suite nous leur serrerons la main. **Cette main ils ne vous la refuseront pas. Ils ne vous la refuseront, jamais.**

Les Camarades comprendront la nécessité et la signification de ce que nous leur demandons aujourd'hui.

Ils auront à cœur de nous le prouver aussitôt après lecture de ces quelques lignes.

POUR LA FRANCE !
POUR NOTRE IDEAL !
VIVENT LES FRANCS-TIREURS et PARTISANS FRANÇAIS !

Bien fraternellement.

Le Comité Militaire du F.T.P.F. de la Drôme.

Among André's papers is another tract, one from the FTP that doesn't need much commentary but speaks volumes about what was at stake during the months of the Liberation:

"BETTER TO DIE ON YOUR FEET THAN TO LIVE ON YOUR KNEES"

INTER E.F.   NATIONAL FRONT   1ST REGIMENT

REGION E. 3   FRENCH FORCES OF THE INTERIOR   3RD BATTALION

FRANCS TIREURS PARTISANS FRANÇAIS

Letter to Comrades in the F.T.P.F.

Comrade, in a few days we will travel down into our big cities now that French landing troops have embarked on the complete Liberation of our Homeland.

I know that most of us have had only the most basic Military Training, and yet we must show our French Friends returning to their Native land that we act as a People's Army, an Organized and Disciplined Army. Only on this **condition** can the Army of the Francs-Tireurs et Partisans Français find the position that its fighting Spirit and its sacrifices have earned for it in the French Army of the future.

Although we are always the first to fight, we must acknowledge that our discipline and our propriety toward our superiors leave a great deal to be desired.

We have already and on many occasions explained what we in a position of responsibility in the F.T.P.F mean when we say Discipline. What we want to achieve in our Army is not the Boche form of discipline, but one that is offered willingly, understood, and welcomed by every one of us. We need to know and understand that, unless we obey our officer's Commands, our Army is irrevocably destined to defeat and fragmentation.

You, Comrade, must know that Discipline takes an Army halfway to Victory: **and what a Victory we shall have!!!** A Victory in which every man will be proud to have taken part: the Victory of Freedom over Oppression, the Victory of the People over Terrible Tyrants.

Furthermore, we in the Francs-Tireurs et Partisans Français must not lose sight of the fact that we constitute more than simply the French Forces of the Interior. Other officers who command the Secret Army collaborate with our officers on a daily basis. These officers do not have the same concept as we FTP do of the Army or of discipline. They are likely to be grievously struck by a lack of propriety in your presentation or your salute. All of this, Comrades, will contribute to the opinion that the people of France and its leaders WILL FORM OF US.

And therefore when we ask you to salute and behave appropriately when addressing Officials and Leaders, you will not be performing an act of humiliation or submission; it should be a spontaneous act on your part. You know your Leaders; like most of you, they have experienced long months in the Maquis. If they hold positions of responsibility today, then it is your Trust in them that confers these positions. And so we loved them. Let us respect them today, without diminishing our spirit of genuine Comradeship. Let us salute our leaders, they have not forgotten who they were only a few months ago, and then we will shake them by the hand. **And they will not refuse this handshake.**

All Comrades will understand the importance and significance of what we ask of them today.

They will be determined to prove this to us as soon as they have finished reading these few lines.

FOR FRANCE!
FOR OUR IDEAL!
LONG LIVE THE FRANCS-TIREURS
ET PARTISANS FRANÇAIS!

In brotherhood with you,
The Military Committee of the F.T.P.F. of the Drôme

Thanks to this tract, I learned how swiftly communist FTPs were transformed: after the Allied landing, they wanted to look like a structured and disciplined military force. The tract also describes the relationship between the Resistance in the interior and de Gaulle's headquarters.

De Gaulle hadn't grasped the fact that—after, at best, incompetence or, at worst, the betrayal of the military in 1940 and their almost unanimous rallying behind Pétain— the Resistance was behind him now not *because* he was a general but *despite* his being one. From his perspective, he doubtless had as little respect for the Resistance as it did for him.

The truth is that de Gaulle was less republican than he was military, and when he landed in France with the Free French Forces in 1944, his priority was to restore some order.

One state. One army. One police force.

De Gaulle was aware that this Resistance that had fought the Vichyite state, army, and police wouldn't settle for some straightforward amnesiac restoration; he knew that these FFI, whose dead in combat and from firing squads numbered in the thousands, and the deportees to Ravensbrück, Buchenwald, and Dachau in the tens of thousands, would not tolerate having no recognition for their sacrifice. But in September 1944, all he could envisage as a sign of gratitude was to merge the now four hundred thousand members of the FFI with the "regular" army. Even this he did reluctantly. He would disingenuously ask network leaders, engineers, laborers, or doctors who'd risked their lives, "What's your rank in the army?" And when he attended a parade of thousands of maquisards in Toulouse, he was contemptuous of the FTP-MOI and, in front of their leader, Serge Ravanel, muttered between his teeth, "What a mockery..."

Sometimes—often, in fact—it's not possible both to make history and to understand it. In that summer of 1944, overjoyed to see France gradually being liberated, André could not have had such a complex outlook. Perhaps he hoped that after the war he would join the army at a rank he'd earned. After all, Marseille and Toulon had been liberated a month ahead of American forecasts, and this was down to the FFI. And Jean de Lattre de Tassigny, who had landed in Provence at the head of one hundred thirty thousand men, could not have traveled so quickly up the Rhône Valley had his 1st Army's ranks not been swollen by an influx of FFI troops—to the point that nearly four hundred thousand men entered Lyon.

But André would not see Lyon liberated, nor even Montélimar. By the time Morvan's two hundred men marched through that town on September 2, 1944, his maquis would have had thirty-eight men killed in combat, four shot by firing squad, and three declared missing, and of the twenty or so who were deported, half would die in the camps. In all, that was fifty-four dead, more than one maquisard in five.

All of them have their name in marble somewhere.

May I say, General, that dying at the age of twenty for freedom, for a "certain idea" of France—that is not a mockery.

The Elfte

READERS BORED BY MILITARY FACTS should skip this chapter. To everyone else I'll confess that I discovered panzers at the age of seven or eight.

I was on a class trip to a military museum that had miniature reconstructions of some of the great battles, many of them French defeats, from Agincourt to Waterloo, which means it was an English museum. At the time I was a pupil in the elementary classes at the Wallington Public School for Boys near London, and I imagine that my merciless British classmates poked fun at this "frog" whose utterly pitiful country lost every battle, unless it capitulated first.

Each English victory was allocated its own room. The low lighting magnified the atmosphere in the theater of war re-created on a large rectangular board measuring perhaps two by three meters and lit with pool table lights. At the age we were, our eyeline was on a level with the terrain: the muddy plain of Agincourt, surrounded by forests of trees made of green foam, was impressive with its hundreds of crossbows, its mounted soldiers and infantrymen. For added realism, loudspeakers played a soundtrack of soldiers' cries, cavalcades, and orders barked by warlords.

Two naval battles had also been depicted: Trafalgar, of course, but most strikingly the 1588 Battle of Plymouth, where Sir Francis Drake dealt fatal blows to the "Invincible Armada" when Philip II of Spain tried to invade England with his galleons. The room was steeped in half darkness, the sea was made of gleaming resin, and dozens of little boats confronted one another in the gloom with tiny luminous flashes erupting from their minute cannons like something in a seascape by Constable; the soundtrack played the howling storm, the roar of salvos, and the sailors' cries. It was good.

But let's get back to our panzers.

The effort put into representing the movements of armored vehicles was exceptional, so much so that there's every possibility the curator or one of his assistants had served in this branch of the services twenty-five years earlier.

I remember three battles in the museum involving armored vehicles. One showed the first rudimentary, brutalist-looking tanks from the Great War, but in that particular room the model maker had taken the most pleasure in sculpting the modeling clay into trenches with their sentry boxes and bunkers, and in representing a deadly assault amid the barbed wire.

This was less inspiring than the next scene, which was set in the dunes of the Sahara Desert and where—wonder of wonders!—some of the damaged tanks submerged in sand gave off a thin thread of acrid smoke every ten minutes. This of course was the Battle of El Alamein, with the victory of Montgomery's Grant tanks over the hitherto unassailable Panzer IIs of Rommel's Afrikakorps.

The setting for the third reconstruction was the taiga, with snow and the rubble of a ruined city. It was clearly Stalingrad. No British troops had been involved, but the decision makers at the museum had most likely wanted to celebrate the heroism of the Russian resistance and demonstrate the power of their heavy T-34s. Here too, a plate referenced the formidable panzers, the brand-new Tigers paralyzed by the Russian winter.

With or without frozen fuel, "panzer" remained a name to be feared, one that crackled like cannon fire. When I discovered that it came from the old French word *pansière*, a piece of medieval armor that protected the *panse*—the belly— Rommel started to look more like Rabelais's blundering giant Pantagruel and to lose a good deal of his daunting presence.

I came away from that museum fascinated by armored vehicles. For several weeks I made drawings of battles between gray and ocher tanks, particularly as—I'll admit— tanks with their caterpillar tracks and guns were a lot easier to draw than a man on horseback. I don't know how those mechanical monsters fired my imagination quite so much, but it's an acknowledged fact that war games and representations of battle constitute an outlet for a child's aggressiveness and can, in their own way, exorcize thoughts of death. Fair enough. In any event, not long afterward, I caught some very active tadpoles in a pond and brought them back in a jar, and that was the end of the tanks. My potential career as a general or arms dealer was nipped in the bud by the extraordinary agitation of a few frog larvae.

I lost interest in panzers for a while. But, as a teenager, my commitment to antifascism led me to read a lot—about Nazism, antisemitism, and German militarism. The Wehrmacht's irresistible power, which demonstrated the effectiveness of Evil, reinforced my repulsion for the regime, and panzers had been its incarnation since the Blitzkrieg. They were also a symbol in steel and gunfire of how unprepared the French had been, and of a complicity among the general staff that sometimes came close to treason, or of their incompetence, which Georges Clemenceau summarized with a still famous quip: "If the generals are so stupid, it's because they're selected from among the colonels."

The French wanted peace, and the Germans were readying for war: the former came up with the Maginot Line and the latter found ways around it, inventing with that first invasion of Poland the victorious alliance among aviation, artillery, and swift-moving armored vehicles.

I'm repeating myself, but never mind: on the corner of the chemin des Lièvres in Grignan is a marble plaque with these words:

"On August 22, 1944, in the Pommier neighborhood near Grignan, German tanks ambushed a file of maquisards from the 'Morvan' maquis that was heading to Montélimar, and they killed six Resistance fighters: Aimé Benoît, André

Chaix, Gabriel Deudier, Jean Gentili, Robert Monnier, and Jean Barsamian. Paul Martin and Raoul Dydier were also killed."

The tanks that killed André Chaix and his companions were from the 11th Panzer Division. The 11th, the *Elfte*, also bore the name of "Ghost Division," *Gespensterdivision* in German, because its speed meant it could pop up where its enemy least expected. Its emblem is a ghost with a skull for a head, brandishing a broadsword and mounted on wheels—a sort of macabre Nazi skateboarder. I also discovered, although it didn't surprise me, that there are people who look back nostalgically at the heyday of the 11th Panzer Division, a Facebook group with one thousand followers glorifies it, and you can buy mugs and T-shirts branded with this ghost symbol.

The *Elfte* had already distinguished itself in the east during Operation Barbarossa, which saw Hitler invade the USSR without declaring war; the division fought in Rostov in November 1942, then in Kursk in August 1943. In the latter battle, Hitler ordered that Germany unleash all its remaining attack potential on the Soviets. It would be in vain, and it would be his downfall. Since Stalingrad, Germany had no longer been on the offensive, and after Kursk, it could no longer win the war.

Streamrollered out of Ukraine by the Red Army in the winter of 1944, almost annihilated in the Battle of the Korsun-Cherkassy Pocket, short of manpower, and with a large proportion of its tanks abandoned or destroyed on the front, the 11th Panzer Division received orders to retreat to near Bordeaux in France. There it received an influx of fresh troops and now comprised a motley contingent of veterans and very young men, teenagers in some cases, recruited from the *Hitlerjugend*, the Hitler Youth, into which—since 1939—all young Germans had been enrolled and from which the German general staff was now liberally helping itself. The division also included Italian, Yugoslav, Polish, Ukrainian, and, to use the Nazi term, "Mongol" recruits—the scant, battered remnants of armies from Eastern nations occupied by the Axis.

This entirely rejuvenated *Elfte* received new equipment, Panzer IVs, armored vehicles from Slovakian Skoda factories, as well as armored cars, and even spanking new Tiger tanks made by Porsche—all in anticipation of Allied landings on the French Riviera.

On paper and at the beginning of the war, a Panzer Division could line up three hundred combat tanks and fifteen thousand men, almost all in vehicles. But on August 13, 1944, faced with the Allies' imminent invasion, when its commander, General von Wietersheim, received orders to leave Rouffiac and head toward Nîmes and Arles, then the Drôme, the 11th was reduced to just twenty-five heavy panzers, as many lighter tanks, eighteen pieces of artillery, and four thousand men, not all of them in vehicles.

This may well be why, when the Allies finally landed in Cannes, Nice, and Saint-Tropez on the morning of August 15, 1944, they suffered only small losses: ninety dead compared to one hundred times as many during the Normandy landings of June 6. They no longer had much to confront. The German Army had retreated toward the Rhine to defend its frontier. If Hitler was abandoning the South of France, it was also because his war machine was low on fuel.

But in the final few weeks, violence against the Resistance intensified. It was not the 11th that was entrusted with the attack on the Vercors maquis on July 21, but a battalion of the 9th Panzer Division that had come from Lyon, supported by battalions of "Mongols" and some *Feldgendarmerie* units. No, the 11th Panzer had a still more difficult task: to protect the left flank of the 19th Army as it retreated toward the Ardennes. Because at this point both the 6th Corps of the U.S. Army and General de Lattre's French Army were pushing north toward Lyon. In fact, the 11th even had to act swiftly to avoid being split in two by Patton's 3rd Army, which liberated Orléans and was advancing eastward, also toward Lyon. But the 11th Panzer's first combat in France would be with the French Resistance in the Drôme, starting on August 20, 1944.

We won't describe in these pages the "Battle of Montélimar" that began on August 24 and that André wouldn't see. We will simply recall that on August 22, a convoy of German tanks was heading north along the chemin des Lièvres in Grignan, followed by an armored car. Driving toward them was an FTP detachment from the Morvan 3rd Battalion, which would form a front. In one of those trucks, alongside twelve other maquisards, was André.

On the side of his truck, one word had been written in white paint: "Hope."

André's Death

"THE LINGERING SIGHS as autumnal violins weep... I repeat ... The lingering sighs as autumnal violins weep...

"Lull my heart in steady, dreamy sleep... I repeat... Lull my heart in steady, dreamy sleep..."

This is an English translation of Verlaine's poem "Autumn Song," which the Radio London announcer Franck Bauer read out in French at nine fifteen on the evening of June 5. But the words had been slightly tweaked: this version of the poem had "autumnal violins" and "lull" where Verlaine's original has "the violins of autumn" and "wound." On the night of June 5 to 6, the night of a full moon, British and American fleets left Portsmouth Harbor for Normandy.

After the first stanza of "Autumn Song" was broadcast on June 1, the broadcast of the second was the signal, but it was just one of many signals for Operation Overlord. It was addressed to one particular armed group, the Sologne Ventriloquist network that would sabotage the railroads. That same evening, the Resistance would hear more than two hundred targeted messages, from "Gentlemen, place your bets" to "I don't like blanquette of veal" and the no less famous "The carrots are cooked."

London was sending orders to all the maquis in France to unleash guerrilla warfare everywhere. A thousand railroad routes were cut off in a matter of days. The Allies wanted to mobilize the German armies on the French interior front, to contain them wherever possible and disrupt communications. In the east, an eleven-year-old boy named Pierre Rosenstiehl—a future mathematician and member of Oulipo—played the nocturnal game of "*va-que-je-t'embrouille*" (get-you-in-a-muddle), which involved swiveling signposts at crossroads and sending Wehrmacht convoys zigzagging in every direction.

In the Drôme region, the maquis from Vercors and La Lance, along with FFI companies from Nyons, launched several offensives. But the Mediterranean landings weren't yet on the agenda. They wouldn't happen until a month later. The maquis weren't adequately equipped to confront a seasoned German Army and its panzer divisions. After a few deadly offensives, they received orders to hold back and wait.

Allied troops finally landed on August 15. Two-thirds of them were Moroccans, Algerians, and Senegalese, soldiers from French-speaking colonized countries coming to liberate France, which was still seen as the "homeland." The German Army retreated along the Rhône, and on the 22nd, Montélimar became the military prize. André was in Sahune, a village to the east of Grignan, where the maquis had some forty maquisards under the leadership of Marius. There was another battalion at La Roche-Saint-Secret, not far from La Paillette to the south. The two Morvan groups were mobilized: André climbed into a truck with some fifteen of his comrades, a car drove ahead of them, and the two units joined forces at Pont-au-Jas in Taulignan. From there they drove toward Montélimar, passing through Grignan. They formed a convoy of two cars and two trucks as they turned onto the Chemin des Lièvres. It was a slight detour, but the bridge over the Chalerne had been cut off.

The small convoy turned the corner at the col du Colombier. At the far end of the road, fifty meters from them, a tank of the 11th Panzer Division in a rearguard position was waiting for them.

It was an Sd.Kfz. 250, one of those light, six-wheeled armored vehicles, which looks from the front not unlike a big friendly tractor and from the back like a nasty little tank. The machine guns in its pivoting gun turret opened fire, and their firepower far outweighed what the maquisards could resist with their rifles and pistols. Three died of bullet wounds, four were seriously injured, and the first truck was struck and went up in flames. The survivors scattered, the German tank called it a day, left its ambush position, and joined the convoy of tanks heading toward Montélimar, where the decisive battle was playing out.

André was very seriously injured. With one leg almost torn off, the poor boy hauled himself to Salles-sous-Bois, where he was found under the trees. He'd tried to make a tourniquet with his shirt. One of his arms had also been hit, the wounds were deep, and he was losing a lot of blood. Dieulefit's mechanic, who was driving past in his van, took him to the hospital in Valréas with other wounded men, covering them with branches and foliage to hide them. André's parents were informed, and they were very soon there, watching over him. One of his friends from the maquis stayed with Jean and Marcelle as they wept.

While André lay groaning on his bed, he was almost certainly told that it was fine, he'd pull through. He was already unconscious. And if he was conscious, he was frightened.

In every language in the world, hope is said to be the last thing to die, *die Hoffnung stirbt zuletzt.*

On the evening of August 23, André Chaix died.

The Name on the Wall

I DON'T KNOW who wrote ANDRÉ CHAIX on the wall; nor do any of the people I was able to ask. The Chaix family had lived in their bakery while the coaching inn had been the blacksmith's home, but only until the 1930s. A low wall and a wrought-iron fence now separate the former coaching inn from the road, but they are only twenty years old. It could have been anyone at any time.

The wall faces the school, but I can't see André himself carving his name, even as a child. Before he died, perhaps Simone or, earlier still, an infatuated girl? Why not? After, though, who? Simone wouldn't have wanted to suffer any more by carving her pain onto a wall. A fellow maquisard maybe. But why, given that with his name on the memorial, his sacrifice would soon be there for all to see? His brother, Marcel, in a desperate bid to cast a spell in late August 1944? I find this plausible and can picture Marcel crying with rage as he carves out each letter.

But of course, I don't know.

What I do know is that, without that name carved on a wall, without André Chaix as my plumb line, I wouldn't have known how to explore an age when generosity and courage lived so unusually side by side with selfishness and despicable behavior. I would never have come so close to men such as Henri Roché and women such as Marguerite Soubeyran, both of whom had remarkable faith in humankind.

I'll never know what a childhood home is, and I will come to terms with this ignorance, which, I realize, is my way of grieving an impossible longing for a line of descent. I make my way through life with no ancestry and no roots. A sort of willful orphan in spite of himself, and no form of belonging would have protected this orphan from the obvious vanity of it all. When my son was born I was the age that André Chaix would have been when I myself was born. Born in 1924 and dead at the age of twenty, André stands in my mind halfway between the image of a father and the reality of a son, but that still doesn't make him a brother, and I can't include him in the family I didn't have. And yet, in writing this book, I was able to think of André alive rather than dead.

Perhaps, André, I wanted to tame your name on the wall because I could no longer be indifferent to it. I wanted it to stop being a complete stranger's name. I hope I haven't burglarized your memory, and I thank everyone who trusted me and described a young man whom most of them didn't even know but had heard of.

I didn't have extravagant ambitions to bring you back to life, André. You will forever be twenty years, two months, and thirty days old, and that's as it should be. A little earlier today, I was once again standing looking at those letters carved into the greige render, and I think I wanted to lend some meaning to the way I looked at it so that I could always give a brotherly smile to your name on the wall.

Bibliography

ON THE RESISTANCE IN THE DRÔME
AND AT DIEULEFIT

Association of the Maquis Morvan. *Maquis et bataillons Morvan.* Imprimerie Lamy, 1987.

Balliot, Pierre. *La Drôme dans la guerre.* De Borée, 2012.

Croyet, Jérôme, and Stéphane Lavit. *La 11e Panzerdivision.* Histoire & Collections, 2022.

Harding, Ganz A. *Ghost Division: The 11th "Gespenster" Panzer Division and the German Armored Force in World War II.* Stackpole Books, 2016.

La Picirella, J. Collectif Valréas, *Témoignages sur le Vercors,* 14th edition. Imprimerie Rivet, 1991.

Lavit, Stéphane, and Vincent Sniprat. *La Bataille de Montélimar.* Histoire & Collections, 2020.

Martin, Patrick-André. *La Résistance dans le département de la Drôme, 1940–1944.* Paris IV Sorbonne university thesis, 2001.

Pennetier, Claude. *Dictionnaire biographique, movement ouvrier, mouvement social.* Les Éditions de l'Atelier—Éditions Ouvrières, 2012.

Suchon-Fouquet, Sandrine. *Résistance et liberté. Dieulefit, 1940–1944.* Presses universitaires de Grenoble, 2010.

Vallaeys, Anne. *Dieulefit, ou le miracle du silence.* Fayard, 2008.

Credits

PHOTO CREDITS

Photos of André Chaix and his friends and family that come from the Anacr archives and Christiane Jouve's personal collection are reproduced by kind permission of Béatrice Jouve and Philippe Biolley (Drôme provençal committee of the Anacr) and of Christiane Jouve.

P. 10: © Yves Bichet; p. 17: © Montjoux-drôme.fr; p. 54: www.11emepanzer.fr; p. 59: © USHMM, Courtesy collection Michael O'Hara; p. 81: © Droits réservés; p. 89: © Everett Collection, Inc. / Alamy Stock Photo; p. 97: Emmanuel Mounier, Pierre Seghers, Pierre Emmanuel in Dieulefit, 1943, photographs by Pierre Lachenal © Archives Éditions des Trois Collines / IMEC; p. 99: cartespostales.com; p. 112: Wikipedia Commons; p. 117: www.memoire-drome.com; p. 123: Amicale du Maquis Morvan, Maquis and Morvan battalions, Imprimerie Lamy, 1987; p. 143: © Bundesarchiv, Bild 1011-722-0416-02 / photographer: Wörner. Other photographs were taken by the author.

p. 5: Seneca the Younger, *Epistles*, XCV, trans. Richard M. Gummere, The Loeb Classical Library (Cambridge, MA: Harvard University Press, 1917), 77: 86–87.

p. 7: Franz Kafka, *Letters to Friends, Family, and Editors* (New York: Schocken Books, 1977), 16.

p. 55: Jean-Paul Sartre, "Paris Alive: The Republic of Silence," *The Atlantic*, December 1944.

p. 60: Victor Klemperer, *I Will Bear Witness: The Nazi Years, 1933–1941*, trans. Martin Chalmers (NY: The Modern Library, 1998), 306.

p. 64: Primo Levi, *If This Is a Man* (currently published in the United States as *Survival in Auschwitz: The Nazi Assault on Humanity*), trans. Stuart Woolf (NY: Orion Press, 1959), 123.

p. 79: Walter Benjamin, *The Arcades Project*, trans. Howard Eiland and Kevin McLaughlin (Cambridge, MA: Harvard University Press).

pp. 79–80: "La Tour Eiffel est toujours là," lyrics by Marc Lanjean and François Llenas, music by Marc Lanjean, © Èditions Salabert, 1942, trans. Adriana Hunter.

p. 109: *Le Chant des partisans*, lyrics by Maurice Druon and Joseph Kessel, music by Anna Marly, © Èditions Raoul Breton, 1945, trans. Adriana Hunter.

p. 111: Italo Calvino, "Il Paradosso," from *Rivista di cultura giovanile*, 23–24, 1960, trans. Adriana Hunter, from the author's translation.

p. 111: Italo Calvino, "Oltre il ponte," words by Italo Calvino, music by Sergio Liberovici, translation found online

at: https://lyricstranslate.com/en/oltre-il-ponte-beyond-bridge
.html. These last two are reproduced by kind permission of
the Wylie Agency.

Acknowledgments

Philippe Berrard, Yves Bichet, Philippe Biolley, Magali Guérin-Chazaud (Drôme regional archives), Mark Hancock, Béatrice Jouve, Christiane Jouve, Huguette Julien, Line Julien, Francis Laurent, Pascal Ory, Micheline Peyrol, and Catherine Verliac (CNC).

HERVÉ LE TELLIER is a writer, journalist, mathematician, food critic, and teacher. He has been a member of the Oulipo group since 1992 and one of the "papous" of the famous France Culture radio show. He has published numerous books of stories, essays, memoir, and novels, including the Goncourt Prize–winning *The Anomaly*, which has sold more than one million copies worldwide, *All Happy Families, Eléctrico W,* and *Enough About Love.*

ADRIANA HUNTER studied French and Drama at the University of London. She has translated more than ninety books, including Marc Petitjean's *The Heart: Frida Kahlo in Paris* and Hervé Le Tellier's *The Anomaly* and *Eléctrico W,* winner of the French-American Foundation's 2013 Translation Prize in Fiction. She lives in Kent, England.